CON ͟ ͟ ͟

A NOTE ON THE AUTHOR

Although Gretta Mulrooney was born in London her parents came from Cork and Offaly. She took a degree in English at the University of Ulster and taught in Dublin. She now lives in England where she works as a social worker. She has published several short stories and her first novel was short-listed for the East Midlands Arts/Heinemann Award. *A Can of Worms* is her first book for children.

1

The Conspiracy

I was in a bad mood. This was definitely a stressful time. My dad and gran were trying to turn me into a laughing-stock. You don't need that when you're fourteen. They might as well have taken me down to the seafront and thrown rotten eggs and tomatoes at me. "Roll up! Roll up and watch Clare being made a fool of!"

I groaned and pulled the pillow over my face as I thought of what Nuala Dunne would say. *She* was going skiing in Zermatt. She'd had her hair permed because the wind and sun would play havoc with it. When she heard about my holiday destination she'd roll her eyes and mouth "Gruesome!"

I punched the pillow and came up for air. Through my window I could see the blue-grey outline of mountains. I was looking at the Mournes and I was mournful. I wished that I could go to sleep and wake up in another body.

I'd known for weeks that Gran was planning to go to Brussels at Easter. She's always checking her passport and applying for visas. If you think that grannies are tiny, dithery old ladies who sit in rocking chairs crocheting cushion-covers then you're in for an eye-opener! My gran's seventy-six and five feet eleven. She swims every day and does Tai-Chi exercises before breakfast.

The first thing you need to know about my gran is that she's very—how can I put it?—outspoken. She's got lots of *opinions* about things. The trip to Brussels was being organised by Action For Pensioners. Gran's on the committee and in between hiking around the globe she attends meetings. She writes long letters to politicians in red ink and goes on cross-border community jaunts to discuss the problems of old people. You may have seen her on telly, at the Taoiseach's office or outside the City Hall in Belfast. She was the tall woman wearing a pink-and-purple track suit with hennaed hair done in a bun. She was probably holding a banner saying something like:

We've Given You Our Best. Now Give Us Yours!

Action For Pensioners often hits the headlines. The last time they made the front pages of the newspapers was when they made an evening raid on one of Dublin's poshest hotels. Six of them swept into the packed dining-room and pointed out that the prices charged for three-course meals were more than an average weekly pension. "Shocked Diners Get Indigestion" was one headline. There was a picture of Gran waving a menu in front of an embarrassed woman's nose and one of a waiter backed up against a door by a man on crutches. I don't think many people enjoyed their meal that night.

It's hard going sometimes at school when Gran's been on telly. I get asked what it's like being related to a superstar. Nuala Dunne sticks her nose in the air and says that it's much nicer to grow old gracefully but Gran says that's code for, "Get lost and be grateful for crumbs from the table!" Anyway, I've seen Nuala's granny at the shops with her knickers round her ankles. The police are always having to take her home when she wanders out on a shop-lifting spree. (She gets away with the thieving because her memory's gone and no-one wants to be seen persecuting an old lady who can't control her elastic.)

The second thing you need to know about Gran is that she's been living in a summerhouse at the end of our garden for six months. She came up from Dublin to Newcastle when my mum left (Mum's her daughter). "I'll have to do something with that child," she wrote in a letter to Dad that I sneaked a look at. "You just haven't got the enthusiasm she needs." She got Dad to put some heating in the summerhouse and raided Oxfam in Belfast for curtains. The place was transformed and cosy within a month. Dad had been saying for years that he'd do it up so that we could rent it out but he'd only managed to mend the holes in the roof. Mum used to give him a knowing look and tap her foot when he'd say he'd get round to it soon....

My friends find Gran fascinating. I suppose it's not surprising. Whereas their grannies give them knitted scarves and socks for their birthdays, mine gives me things like Malaysian bird-calling pipes or Norwegian goat-bells. When friends call round, Gran doesn't say, "Take your shoes off, you'll mark the carpet," or "You'll catch a cold coming out with wet hair." She tells them that Europeans smell very peculiar to Chinese people or that the best treatment for dysentery is yogurt or that she had a tasty plate of chocolate ants in Lima.

I hadn't taken much notice of the trip to Brussels. It was never easy to keep track of what Gran might be up to next. I knew that a coach had been organised and that it was a big international event. Hundreds of old people were going to head for Brussels to protest to the European Commission about crummy pensions. I'd heard Gran on the phone talking to her pensioner mafia in Dublin, Belfast and London. I could tell from the strong smell of poster paints in her room and the coloured smudges on her nose from when she got too close to the paper that she'd been beavering away on publicity. So I knew it was all being planned. What I didn't know was that I'd be going with them!

To reveal the core of the story, as Miss Casey, my English teacher says, I have to tell you that this treachery was plotted while I was at school.

I arrived home on that fateful Tuesday afternoon to find that Gran and Dad had stitched me up. You know how sometimes you just want the world to go away? I'd had a rotten day and I was looking forward to getting home and making a huge orange slush and three choc-spread sandwiches with no one to bother me or pass a witty remark like, "Have some bread with your chocolate, Clare."

It had been an extra rotten day because:

1 My apple pudding had failed to rise and was lying like a soggy mop at the bottom of my bag;

2 My running shoes were too small and had pinched my toes. A blister was starting to throb on the back of my heel for good measure;

3 I'd had to put up with Mary Conway in Chemistry and she's got breath like mouldy haddock;

4 The Maths teacher had remembered to give us homework.

As I struggled into the house, balancing my cooking disaster, my homework folder and my sports bag, I heard voices. My dad doesn't usually come in from his smelly garage till gone six and Tuesday was Gran's afternoon for her art class. My heart sank as I realised that he and Gran were in the kitchen. Now I wouldn't be able to play my records full-blast or borrow Dad's dumb-bells to work on my biceps. I looked at the plastic motto that Dad had nailed up in the hall: "It Never Rains but It Pours." Too true, I thought. The hall stank of Gran's extra-strong, hand-rolled Cuban cigars. I coughed loudly in protest. I've read about passive smoking.

"Hallo, Clare, love," Gran bawled. "Guess what treat we've got for you?"

I thought hopefully: a new bike, some cassettes, the sweatshirt I'd been dropping heavy hints about. I went into the kitchen, thinking that the day was looking up.

"Hallo," I said, "what is it, then? What's the treat?"

Dad rolled his eyes. I thought he looked queasy, as he did when Mum left.

"What is it? Come on," I urged, getting the bread out.

"Well..." My dad was staring at the wall as if he'd only just noticed it was painted cream. Somehow he didn't look as if he was going to give me exciting news.

"Well, your gran was offering—and I think it would be a good idea...she was saying she could take you...and it would be an experience...." His voice trailed as if his battery had faded.

"Take me where?" This was making me nervous. I spread an extra inch of chocolate goo on my sandwich.

Gran took a deep puff on her cigar and looked me in the eye. "Your dad's got a lot of work booked for Easter," she said, "and I've arranged to take you to Brussels. Your dad thinks you won't want to go but I've told him you'll jump at the chance."

Jump over a cliff more like, I thought. My sandwich was hovering in the air near my mouth. "Brussels?" I croaked, "on the wrinklies' trip?"

"The Action For Pensioners expedition," Gran corrected. "Don't let them hear you call them wrinklies—they'll have your guts for garters. It's all sorted—Dan Burke's grandson has got you a reduction. It'll only cost your dad twenty pounds."

"But..." My jaw had locked. My stomach felt as heavy as the doomed apple-pud. Dad was gazing at me pleadingly with a look that said, "Don't make a fuss please humour me just this once you know I've got a heavy workload you'll hurt your gran's feelings if you refuse to go and anyway you'll have to because I won't be here."

"Heavens," Gran said, "you look as if you've been

offered a week down the salt-mines. I'm not that awful, am I?"

Now that's the sort of adult question you just can't answer. Whatever you say will hurt the other person's feelings. I thought of all the things I could do to avoid going. They flashed through my mind like a fast-forward film:

- Lock myself in my room with a supply of choc-spread sandwiches until Gran had gone.
- Run away from home.
- Develop a contagious illness.
- Hide on the ferry and come straight back.

"It'll be good fun, pet," Dad said with a feeble smile. "Just think, your first time abroad!"

Oh yes, I could see myself boasting about it at school: "A luxury trip with the over-sixties. Plenty of room for walking-sticks and free batteries for hearing-aids. No expense spared—false teeth provided!" My reputation was going to be ruined when this got out. I might as well wear a badge saying "Weirdo." Gran had often said that she'd take me on holiday with her one day but I'd imagined Spain or Greece. Beach discos had been my dream, not bingo with the ancient.

I wanted the ground to open, the sky to fall, World War III to be declared. I wanted to shout and scream. I wanted a dad like Nuala Dunne's who worked in an office, came home with clean fingernails and earned pots of money. I wanted a gran who stayed in her rocking-chair, crocheting and not being a nuisance. Much as I loved her, at that moment I wished that she would dematerialise and be beamed to another planet. I stared at her hard, hoping to make her vanish through willpower, but she and Dad kept looking at me expectantly.

"Just think of the people and places you'll see," Dad said.

"I'm not going," I muttered. "It's no good trying to get round me; it'd be horrible."

Dad raised his shoulders. "I wouldn't pass up the experience," he said in a hurt voice. "It's not every girl who gets this kind of offer."

"No," I snapped, "other girls get to go to Euro-Disney and the Alps. *You* go if you think it's so good. I'd be surrounded by doddery old dears wanting me to carry their cases and help them open their pills." I knew I shouldn't say things like that, especially in front of Gran, but I didn't care—they shouldn't have ganged up on me. "There'd be nothing to do," I added, chucking the rest of my dying sandwich away. Somehow I didn't feel hungry any more. "Everyone will be tucked up in bed by eight o'clock. I'd be bored to death."

There was silence for a few minutes. Dad rubbed at the tablecloth and whistled under his breath. Gran lit up another cigar and picked a dangling shred of tobacco from her lip.

"Well," she said, blowing a smoke ring, "I never thought you were so unadventurous, Clare. You youngsters are such stick-in-the-muds."

"Clare, please..." Dad tried winking at me.

"No!" Gran stopped him, waving her hand. "Don't

insist. If Clare hasn't the gumption for the challenge I don't want her along. She can stay at home on her own instead of sailing across the sea and living life. When I was her age I couldn't wait to strike out. I nagged my poor father to let me take off to the Continent!"

Now she'd made me feel guilty. I knew I'd hurt her feelings. I thought of all the times she'd taken me out when Dad was working or sunk in depression because of Mum. Gran has a spark that makes her seem younger than some people my own age. She says it's because she was widowed early and she was too busy making a go of things to get "middle-aged and boring." (She always glances at Dad when she makes that remark.) I thought of what it would be like being stuck with my tired, grumpy father over Easter. The outdoor swimming-pool wouldn't be open yet and my two closest friends were going to be away. It's all very well living by the coast but after a while one wave looks very much like another.

I looked at my dad, slouching at the table, grinding sugar grains with a teaspoon. No wonder Mum left. He even grinds his teeth. She went off to Donegal to join a community that meditates. She read about them in a magazine at the hairdresser and vanished a few days later. I've often wondered what she meditates about. We had one postcard from her, a view of Bloody Foreland. It said, "At last I have found true harmony with the earth, Halcyon." (That's the name the community gave her. I looked it up; it's a Greek word meaning "calm." Mum must have changed a lot—she used to be a frantic nail-biter.)

I've always felt that I had a less than fair start in life

with a father who's obsessed with greasy engines and a mother who turned into Halcyon. I owed it to Gran that I wasn't called Artemis. (Mum had been on a holiday in Greece the year before I was born.) Gran managed to talk her out of it. I looked at her from under my eyelids, thinking that if it hadn't been for her, I'd have been a laughing stock for the whole of my life. She wanted to make me one for only a few days.

I sighed loudly. "OK," I said grudgingly, "I'll go."

Dad beamed with relief and put a grateful kiss on my cheek. Mrs Dwyer had been discussing Judas in class that very morning. I knew that Dad would try to get pally later on to make up for the fact that he was sending his only child off with a group of old wrecks to a foreign shore. He'd probably suggest chips for supper—his idea of big spending.

"We'll have to get you a passport," Gran said, standing up and brushing ash from her tracksuit. "We'll be going via Dublin and we'll meet up with a British contingent at Dover. Ugh!" She pointed at my bag. "What's that?"

A green sludge was oozing across the floor.

"That's my apple pudding," I said. "It's been that kind of day."

***

2

Sniffs, Sobs and Solutions

I woke up the morning after the plot had been revealed feeling like a teddy bear that's lost its stuffing. I am being forced to spend Easter in a city that sounds like a vegetable, I told myself, as I plodded to the bathroom and looked at myself pityingly in the mirror.

When I'd dressed, I took a peek at the photo of Mum that I keep in the drawer under my bed. "Do you know what they're doing to your daughter?" I asked her, but she just smiled back at me. She met Dad when her car broke down outside Newry, after she'd been to a weekend course on holistic massage in Belfast. Dad turned up with his breakdown truck, fixed her alternator and took her for a drink. They got married a month later. In those days, apparently, he had a way with words.

I put a black ribbon in my hair as a sign of protest against the wrong that had been done to me. I knew that

Gran would say, "Nothing's ever as bad as it seems," but she didn't have problems like mine. Gran's got lots of sayings: "The meek won't inherit the earth; they'll get buried under it"; "A busy mind is a happy mind." When Mum left and Dad was looking blotchy she told him, "When the going gets tough, the tough get going." She also gave him a cigar and said, "It takes two to tango." (Whatever that means. I don't recall them ever going dancing.)

As I went downstairs I heard the thump of the letterbox and saw a huge pile of mail landing on the doormat. There were another couple of dozen of the letters that Gran gets from all over the world—Delhi, Zagreb, Jaffa, Copenhagen. They say things like, "You may remember we met at Niagara Falls and you told me that I could claim money for my sick wife," or "My dear Nora, that cider vinegar solution you recommended for tired eyes worked a treat." Gran doesn't travel to look at the scenery or sunbathe like normal people. She pokes about back streets and flea markets and chats to folk at Tibetan and Siberian bus-stops. (Do they have bus-stops in those places?) She always carries a bag crammed with herbal pills, in case she meets a Tibetan with a runny nose. We get postcards from her with scrawled comments; "Saw Gorby yesterday. He's a chunky hunk." The one from Albania just said, "Bleak!"

She's had some return visitors in the summerhouse. I never know when I might be introduced to Benjamin from Botswana or Carlotta from Caracas. Sometimes, when several of them turn up at once, the place looks like an international refugee camp. Rucksacks block the door and Tooraloo, Gran's filthy-tempered cat, looks very put-out.

We take them for walks up Slieve Donard and they say never mind; they like the Irish rain.

I dragged myself to school with a nasty dark cloud squatting over my head and spent all morning waiting for it to burst. During maths I dozed off for a few minutes and had a horrible daymare; Nuala Dunne and a couple of my (former) friends were standing by the coach, waving me off to Brussels. They were doubled over with hysterics.

At break, Nuala was going on about her skiing trip and what factor suncream she'd need. I hoped that an Alp would fall on her head. The end of term loomed menacingly; friends would be asking if I had any plans and I'd have to tell them I'd be away. I thought of saying that we were going to visit my Aunt Ellen in Dublin but if they saw my dad in the street and spoke to him they'd find me out. Shame!

It's embarrassing to have to tell you this, but after lunch—what lunch? I felt so sick I couldn't even face my Nutchoc sandwiches—I started crying at Miss Casey's desk! English is my favourite subject but I'd hardly heard a word she'd said. At the end of the lesson she asked me to stay behind.

"Is something the matter, Clare?" she asked. "You're usually full of beans!"

Beans, sprouts—it was unbearable. You know how sometimes you're trying not to cry but someone asks you what's wrong in a kind, sympathetic voice and the tears just roll? Well...I used twelve of Miss Casey's man-size, triple-strength tissues. She made me sit down and I told her between gulps about Brussels and what it would mean for my image. What I like most about Miss Casey is that she

really listens. She didn't say that it was a wonderful opportunity or that I should be grateful or I was silly to worry
about what people thought. When I'd finished and was
clutching a ball of mangled pulp, she sat back and nodded
thoughtfully. I knew that she'd be "reviewing the situation," because that's what she tells us to do if we have a
problem.

"Right," she said, pulling her chair near me, "let's face
it: you have to go."

"Mmm." I sniffed and nodded.

"And you love your gran—she's great." (Miss Casey
met Gran when she joined us for our "oral history" spot and
told the class about her father's memories of Parnell.)

"Mmm."

"So—you need to make the best of the situation. You
could have fun, you know."

"Maybe, I suppose—but if my friends find out..." I saw
the daymare figures again, jeering and calling. "It's not the
kind of holiday that's got any *credibility*," I moaned.

"Hmm. I might have a solution to that. Yes, it's
coming to me now, I'm having one of my brainwaves!" Miss
Casey was grinning. She gave me a friendly poke on the
shoulder and rummaged in her bag. "Listen," she said,
"fortune is smiling on you after all. This came in a couple of
days ago and I thought of you when I saw it." She pulled out
a glossy leaflet and handed it to me.

"Impressions of Europe—The Challenge for Youth," it
said. I read on, while Miss Casey jiggled up and down in her
chair.

"Are you visiting Europe this year? We want to hear

about your experiences. There are prizes for the successful entries! Send us an account of your holiday. It can be on any subject you like and written in any form. The choice is yours. We're looking for exciting, original views of Europe from its young citizens. So pick up that pen!"

Miss Casey tapped the paper. "The Institute for European Cooperation is organising it," she said. "Look, you get five hundred pounds if you win and the three best entries from Ireland go into a European youth anthology. It's ideal for you, Clare—and it couldn't have come at a better time."

"It looks interesting," I said, "but I don't see how it helps my reputation."

She rubbed her hands and laughed. "That's the clever bit," she said. "I'll tell the class that I've asked you to do it as recognition for coming top in languages again. You'll be going to Brussels, the heart of Europe, as a correspondent. It's a handy coincidence that your gran happens to be going at Easter and can just fit you in with her group at the last minute. Your friends will be dead impressed!"

I stared at her. I wanted to hug her and bring her apples every day for the rest of my life. The cloud above my head lifted and sailed through the open window. I saw it disappear over the tennis courts where Nuala Dunne was playing to tone up her calf-muscles.

"It's brilliant," I said. "It solves everything." I suddenly felt like Shakespeare, Joyce and Betsy Byars rolled into one. There would be no stopping me; I saw myself scribbling away by torchlight, putting gems on paper, capturing the whole of Brussels life. "I'll write the best entry," I declared.

"Modest as always, Clare," Miss Casey said cheerfully,

but I could tell that she was really keen as well by the way she was picking at her nails. "You'll need to give it careful thought," she said, "Brussels doesn't have the reputation of being the most exciting city in Europe. You'll have to find a way of bringing it to life, getting an unusual angle that'll make the judges sit up. Perhaps there'll be a place or an event that you'll be able to dramatise or a character that you'll come across. *Atmosphere* will be important, of course, and *clear* syntax. Above all, don't forget..."

"I know, I know," I interrupted—she's said it so many times—"don't forget, it's got to have legs." (That's her phrase for a story that carries the reader's interest. If she draws a pair of running boots at the bottom of your work, you know you've done well.)

"Good," said Miss Casey. "I think you could turn this into a great opportunity. You see," she nodded, gathering up her books, "even the worst disaster can be reversed. Clouds and silver linings." As she propped the door open she said over her shoulder, "If you win, don't forget who told you about it!"

I walked on air through the playground, thinking it was funny that she should have mentioned clouds. I was stepping on silver now, light-hearted. I yanked the black ribbon from my hair and stuffed it in my pocket. I was suddenly ravenous. I'd be really inventive, I thought, find something to write about that no one else would think of.

Maybe it was just as well that I'd no idea of what I was going to find in Brussels!

***

3

Secret Protests and a Heart Attack

Vive le Channel Tunnel! The Action For Pensioners trip to Brussels (motto: "We fight for the rights of all pensioners everywhere") wasn't very active to start with. The ferry was delayed for four hours at Dover.

Dan Burke (76, from Bray) had already been sick very loudly on the boat from Dublin to Holyhead. He said he knew he should never have crossed the Irish Sea to the land of oppressors and colonisers. Gran told him he'd better tone down his remarks if he didn't want to get into fights.

Ethel McCracken (68, from Coleraine) was having bladder trouble and had to keep making a beeline for the Ladies. Bert Craig (70, from Banbridge) told her she might as well stay in there and save her legs and she told him to go and boil his head. Gran tried to give Ethel essence of nasturtium for her waterworks but she was in such a bad mood she wouldn't take it. Dymphna O'Malley (81, from

Drogheda) only made things worse by offering Ethel a relic of Saint Martin to press to her abdomen.

The crossing was choppy. Several people looked green and wobbly but that may have been because Marie Hanlon (72, from Lucan) brought pilchard-and-pickle sandwiches. Gran and I were okay because we'd taken distilled marigold before sailing. Peggy Crowley (75, from Portlaoise) got her walking stick stuck in the turnstile of the duty-free shop and an enormous queue built up behind her while an assistant tried to wrench it free. Bert Craig bought more than his allowed quota of booze and Gran reminded him sharply that he was expected to stand outside the European Commission — not lie on a stretcher.

Bert was stopped by a customs officer at Ostend and questioned about his clanking bags. He snarled, "Get your filthy Frog hands off me." I didn't think that this was the spirit of European cooperation. Peggy poked at the customs man with her walking stick and he backed off with his hands up. I thought I might get a walking stick; they seemed to come in useful.

I unpacked my bag in the Hotel Orlando in Brussels. The contents reflected the fact that I didn't expect to be rushed off my feet. Apart from one full change of clothes I'd brought:

- Six books: novels and an illustrated history of Egypt;
- A pack of playing cards;
- A tin whistle and instruction book (I'm teaching myself to play.)

- Travelling chess set (I'm going to practise playing against myself so that I can beat Gran.)
- Some exercise books for my witty observations on Brussels life.

I thought that that lot should help me pass three days. I'd already mastered the first eight bars of "Yellow Bird" on the whistle. The next tune, "Frère Jacques," seemed in keeping with the Continental setting.

Gran and I were sharing a room. She was in the bathroom, singing and splashing loudly. I was a bit worried about her; she'd started acting oddly as soon as we reached Ostend. A strange, secretive smile came over her face and she hummed to herself on the coach. I thought maybe it was the distilled marigolds having an unusual effect. I asked her if she was okay and she patted my shoulder and said, "Terrific!"

The hotel was two-star, which meant it was comfy. The corridors smelled of coffee and olive oil. I'd already washed an unmentionable part of myself in the bidet and found a paper bag full of sick stuffed behind the washbasin. Gran tutted and said that the Orlando wasn't what it used to be. When I asked her if she'd stayed here before, she smiled and said, "Oh yes, many years ago."

The hotel was very quiet, just as I thought it would be. There was no swimming-pool, games room or health suite with integral sauna, jacuzzi and whirlpool, as featured in Nuala Dunne's holiday brochure. The rooms didn't even have TV. I tried playing a few bars of a jig on my whistle to cheer myself up.

During dinner I decided that Bert Craig was definitely xenophobic. (Look in your dictionary.) He made a terrible fuss and complained about being served "foreign muck." He'd brought his own bottle of tomato ketchup and slopped it over his Coq Au Vin, turning it an interesting pale blood colour. When he found herbs in the butter he hit the roof and asked what was wrong with plain Irish cooking? Gran told him that he was disgraceful and said she wouldn't have brought him if she'd known he was a petty-minded islander. We were supposed to be forging common bonds with our European neighbours, she reminded him loudly, not creating differences. She got very worked up, waving her fork and swooping her knife through the air as she finished with a rousing cry of, "Liberty, Equality, Fraternity!" The waiters clapped and one of them kissed her hand. The chef came from the kitchen and presented her with a rose.

Bert subsided and kept his face down. His cheeks were the same colour as the rosebuds. He didn't appear to have got the message about Europe and all of us having common interests. He seemed to dwell on the war a lot—everywhere we'd driven through reminded him of it—and he didn't think much of the French and Belgians who'd given in to the Germans. Dan Burke had a chuckle at Bert's expense; Bert had earlier referred to the fact that Dan hadn't fought in the war but patrolled Kildare during the Emergency.

After dinner, we went on a sightseeing tour of Brussels by coach. Ethel went into a sulk and locked herself in her room because Gran told her we couldn't stop for a loo every ten minutes. I thought I might be able to jot down some notes on the sights but I couldn't make much out in the dark. Instead, I played "Yellow Bird" and everyone sang along. I made only two mistakes. Dan Burke turned out to be a hot whistle player and told me it was best to store it in buttermilk before he gave us "The Lonesome Boatman," two hornpipes and "Little Brown Jug." I took the whistle off him after that—the human ear can only stand so much.

When we arrived back at the Orlando the woman at reception told Gran that a message had been left for her. She grabbed the envelope and hurried me to the lift. Up in our room she tore it open and did a dance around the floor while she read it, a sort of hop-and-skip effort.

"Ooh, Clare," she said, "I feel eighteen again!"

"What is it?" I asked, hoping that she'd won the lottery or an exotic holiday for two in the Bahamas. Gran had been a terrible fidget all evening, glancing at her watch every few minutes and humming that tune she'd started at Ostend. She was la-laaing it again. She'd whisked a pillow off the bed and was clutching it in her arms, gliding round the floor like a ballroom dancer. Her hair began to fall out of its bun and her eyes had glazed over. "That's it," I thought, "she's flipped. I'm in charge of a loony grandmother!" I imagined the message I'd have to send Dad: "Gran bananas. Come quickly!"

She was dancing faster and faster, singing a Strauss waltz as she slipped and curved round the beds. "Da da dee dum, da da dee dum, da da dee dum, diddly om pom pom..."

"Gran," I said, putting on my sternest teacher's voice, "stop it immediately! What's happened?"

She whirled by me and caught me up with the pillow,

flipping me across to her bed. I was flumped down while Gran panted, breathless and rosy-faced. She patted at her chest and then started to pace up and down the room.

"Something's happened that I've dreamed about for years," she wheezed, "I've found Philippe!"

I folded my arms and narrowed my eyes. I'd never heard of a Philippe before—maybe he was one of Gran's screwball fellow-travellers. She'd probably met him on the Great Wall of China or in a café in Finland. She was rubbing her arms and shivering. Her eyes were misty and far away.

"Who's Philippe?" I asked impatiently. "One of your correspondents?"

Gran shook her head quickly. "Oh no, not one of those...he's a...a friend I had a long time ago, before I married your grandfather." She clasped her hands and took a breath, pressing her chest in. ("Breathe through the diaphragm to regain serenity," she instructs me.) "You know," she said quietly. "I was in Paris before the war. I taught English conversation for a while."

I nodded. I'd heard her talk about her Paris adventures but I'd never paid much attention. She'd had a part-time job in a school and she'd studied figure drawing at night-class. There was a photo of her on her writing table. She was on a boat on the Seine with a group of friends. They were all wearing jaunty hats and smoking. Her eyes had the same bright, sparkly light as they have now, the one she says I've inherited.

She came and sat on my bed, tidying her hair absent-mindedly. "I met Philippe there," she said, "through a friend called Madeleine. He was Belgian but he was studying history in Paris. I had to go back to Dublin when war was threatening. Philippe joined the Resistance and fought in it throughout the war. He managed to get messages to me a couple of times but then he was wounded in 1944 and we lost contact. I couldn't find out where he'd been taken. I never saw him again. There was terrible chaos at the end of the war, thousands of refugees everywhere, and I couldn't trace him. I came over from Dublin but it was no good. I thought he'd died with millions of others. But now . . . now I've found him!"

She looked like one of those girls in teen magazines, all dewey-eyed and dreamy. They're the kind of pictures that always make me want to go: "Yuk!"

"This letter," she said, "is from Madeleine. We've always kept in contact— you know, Christmas cards and letters down the years. We met up at a demo in Geneva last summer and got talking about old times. I told her how I'd started to think about Philippe again lately. You take stock as you get old; sometimes the past is as real as the present. Maddy's been doing a bit of detective work. She's managed to find Philippe and she's going to take me to see him tomorrow night." She sat up straight, fanning herself with the letter. "I must calm down and think. Will you fetch me my Rescue Remedy?"

I got the bottle and she put three drops on her tongue. I was so tired I was having to pull faces to stop my eyes closing. I took a few drops too, hoping that it would keep me awake. This Philippe business was fascinating. I didn't want to drop off until I had all the details. I pulled a chair up to Gran.

"Was Philippe your boyfriend?" I asked. I like to know exactly what's what.

She winked at me. "Yes. When he realised that the war was definitely going to break out he came home to Brussels. I visited him here for a weekend at this very hotel, just before I left for Ireland. It was the last time I saw him. We seemed to realise that we had to snatch what time we could have together."

This was truly romantic, I thought, looking at the soft gleam in her eyes. Her face had become younger. I'd never thought of Gran having boyfriends and being in love. It was like one of those black-and-white films you see on TV on Sunday afternoons. There are always violins and men with smoothed-down hair. Gran and I usually watch one if it's raining and Dad's working. We get a box of chocs and sprawl on cushions with the gas-fire humming. I could see Gran in a suit with padded shoulders and her hair curled over her forehead, waiting for Philippe in the hotel foyer. He'd have worn a trench coat and had a cigarette dangling from his bottom lip.

"It must have been exciting," I said. "Was it scary, not knowing if you'd see him again?"

Gran stared thoughtfully into space. "Yes, it was, but it felt as if nothing bad could happen to us that weekend. We were like children hiding from the bogeyman and dreaming of happy times ahead. But it wasn't to be."

"Just as well for me, or I wouldn't be here!"

Gran laughed, patting my hand. "Indeed!"

"Was he handsome?" I asked.

"Oh yes, very. And he was a very gentle man. He hated

death and destruction." She squeezed my hand tight. "I've often wondered, as I've travelled, if I might one day come across him; just see him in a café or walking along a street."

"Do you really think you'd recognise him?" I asked. "How old is he?"

"Nearly eighty. I'd always know Philippe, anywhere. He's not the kind of person you forget. I can hardly believe it: after all these years, to find that he's still alive!"

I tried to imagine it. It would be as if I got home to find that Mum had come back and she and Dad had sorted themselves out. I know it probably won't happen but I dream about it sometimes and picture us having dinner in the kitchen like we used to.

I suddenly yawned a huge yawn. Gran looked at her watch and tutted. "Bedtime," she said. "Don't forget, it's the big rally tomorrow."

She was humming again as we got into bed. Every now and then, as I was about to drop off, I'd hear her laugh or sigh softly.

"Go to sleep," I said crossly. "You're keeping me awake."

"Hmm? Oh, sorry pet, it's just..." She hummed under the duvet.

"Gran," I mumbled, drifting off, "what's that tune?"

"Mon Legionnaire", she whispered, "a song by Edith Piaf. Philippe loved it."

Gran was up and dressed before I opened my eyes. When I did I thought that an enormous budgie had flown into the room but it was Gran, wearing a bright yellow tracksuit and red plimsolls. I rubbed my eyes and brought her into focus. She was piling her hair up and securing it with a butterfly clip. She looked ready for anything.

"Come on, lazybones," she said. "Hot chocolate and croissants and then it's off to the Commission. Have you got your banner?"

"It's under the bed."

The banners had been prepared before we left. Mine said:

Pensioners of Europe Unite! Grey Power Is Strong!
Gran's proclaimed:

Once We Fought Wars. Now We Fight for Each Other!

They were eye-catching, in huge black lettering against a red-and-white background. I thought I'd look daft, a fourteen- year-old carrying a banner about grey power and I said so to Gran as I dressed. She wagged her finger at me. "One day you'll reap the benefits of what we sow. Everyone gets old, as sure as night follows day. We're not a different species from you, you know, just because our skin sags and our bladders play up. It's like bread in the oven; you're the dough still proving and I'm a well-done loaf!"

I wanted to laugh but instead I pulled a face. Some- times I'm like that: I do the complete opposite of what I really want to do. I don't know why; it doesn't make me feel good, especially when I think it's Gran I'm annoying.

"Huh!" I said, "I doubt I'll get to seventy-six, what with bombs and pollution and global warming. Maybe I'm the dough that never gets cooked."

Gran gave me one of her knowing looks. "Maybe, maybe not, but as long as there's one day left, it's worth fighting for. Philippe used to say that when he heard that another of his friends had been captured."

Her eyes clouded. I had a sudden feeling that I didn't know anything and I felt stingy and cross with myself. I went to Gran and hugged her.

"Where are you meeting him?" I asked. "Will I be able to see him?"

"Maddy's taking me tonight," she said, "I'll see how it goes." She clutched my hand hard. "What if he doesn't remember me, Clare? What shall I do? I woke up this morning worrying that he might have become forgetful. I couldn't bear that—he was so quick and clever."

It was strange to see Gran nervous and twitchy. I was used to her being the one who acted sensibly and always knew what to do. I tried to look wise.

"You know what you say," I reminded her. "Nothing ventured, nothing gained. He might be a right raver; he might sweep you off your feet and take you to a night-club!"

She laughed. "I don't know who's nuttier, you or me. Here, take some powdered hollyhock; it strengthens the voice."

"Why do we need this?" I asked, swallowing the little white pills.

"We'll be shouting, won't we?" Gran said. "Making ourselves heard by the fat cats of Brussels."

There was quite a gathering outside the European Commission, including wheelchairs and a sea of walking-sticks. (You know, I'd never thought of a walking-stick as a dangerous weapon before but they're really useful for poking, prodding, and whizzing in the air. I think you should have to buy a licence for one.) Groups of pensioners had come from all over Europe: Holland, Ireland, France, Spain, Italy, Great Britain. There was a tremendous din as they argued with Eurocrats and swapped notes about hotels and food.

One old man in a wheelchair was shouting louder than anyone else, in very fast French. He was wearing his army uniform, complete with medals, and looked every inch a soldier except that his legs stopped at the knees. He had a wobbling placard hoisted over the top of his chair. It said, "I Gave My Legs for You; You Give Me Scraps." Bert went up to him and saluted solemnly. The old man gravely returned the salute and then shouted even louder.

Gran had instructed Dan Burke and Bert Craig to hold a banner between them and they both looked as if they'd been given lemons to suck. Dan had been told by a mischief-maker that one of Bert's uncles had been in the Black-and-Tans and he was refusing to speak to Bert. He'd only nod or shake his head or point with his finger and Bert had been heard referring to "bog-trotters." Gran had threatened to wrap the banner round their heads if they didn't shape up.

I'd started off thinking that I'd die of embarrassment. I'd never been on a demonstration before. (I'd missed the young people's peace demo in Belfast because I had flu.) I wedged myself into a corner behind some Spaniards and thought I'd pass the time absorbing local colour for my competition entry. Gran flew off handing out leaflets and badgering men in smart suits who were trying to ignore the fact that hundreds of pensioners were yelling and shaking their fists, handbags and sticks at them. I whistled through my teeth, which is what I do when I'm trying to appear "cool." I whistled the day that Ann Cassidy knocked down a whole shelf of encyclopaedias while I was acting librarian and it worked quite well.

I found that I was whistling the tune that Gran had been driving me insane with. Then I saw that one of the men in suits was waving his hands at Gran as if he was trying to brush away a fly. A policeman stepped forward and clicked his fingers at her. She hopped sideways and continued her argument, pushing a leaflet at the pin-stripe suit. The policeman gave her a shove and some of the leaflets fell out of her hand.

I found myself dumping my banner in the hands of a startled Spaniard and elbowing my way to the front. No one was going to treat my gran like that.

"Hey," I said to the policeman, "lay off. Don't shove old ladies around."

His mouth dropped in astonishment. Pin-stripe suit was chuckling.

"You should pay these people decent pensions," I said loudly. I didn't see what he had to laugh about. "They wouldn't have to come here if they got a fair deal."

A big cheer went up from the crowd around me and I realised that I'd been yelling. Gran was picking up her leaflets but the policeman deliberately trod on some of them and said, "Go 'ome, old woman; go 'ome."

"I've every right to come here and speak my mind," she said, putting her face close to his. "You hadn't even been thought of when we fought for free speech. You're the one who should go home—and remember that we gave you a home to go to!"

The policeman went purple and took out a notebook. "What is your name?" he asked importantly.

"Maud Gonne," said Gran. "What's yours—Adolf Hitler junior?"

"You come with me," said the policeman nastily, grabbing her arm.

She's going to be arrested, I thought. I didn't reckon that this was quite the impression of Europe I was supposed to be getting. I could see the newspaper headlines: "Pension Hooligans Strike at Heart of Brussels," or "Battling Gran Gets Copped!" Gran was hitting the policeman on the arm with leaflets and an old Italian lady was gabbling what sounded like insults and trying to hook him round the ankle with her Zimmer. Just then there was a shattering scream and I heard Peggy Crowley yelling at the top of her voice, "Help! Help, quick! It's his heart!"

Dan Burke was staggering in a circle, clutching his chest and gasping while Peggy danced after him, waving her arms. The crowd drew back as Dan fell to his knees.

"Police! Ambulance! Quick!" bawled Peggy.

The policeman dropped Gran's arm. "Move, move!" he called, making for Dan and reaching for his pocket radio.

I felt my hand being grabbed and before I knew what was happening Gran was hurrying me down a side street and hailing a cab.

"Dan, what about Dan?" I gasped as we fell in.

Gran wiped her brow. "He's all right, he was a diversion."

I stared at her, swallowing. "What? You mean he's not ill?"

"'Course not," she said, winding down a window. "That was tactics. We'd worked it out beforehand, in case there was trouble. We're not daft, you know; we've done lots of these demos!"

"You might have told me," I said, imagining her in a dimly-lit room with a map, drawing up a battle plan.

She shook her head. "Only three of us knew. It's better that way. Careless talk costs lives!"

I knew that was an old wartime motto but I didn't see why Gran had to be so dramatic. "You do exaggerate," I said, annoyed at having been left out. Anyone would think I couldn't be trusted with a secret. First the long-lost Philippe, now this. What else did she have up her sleeve? I shot her a dark look.

"I suppose there are other plots I don't know about," I said in an injured voice.

"Not at the moment," Gran answered sweetly. "Now, we'll stop for a quiet cup of coffee and let the excitement die down." She giggled. "Dan was convincing, wasn't he? He can be a pain but he comes up trumps when you need him."

* * *

4

An Old Banger, an Old Boyfriend
and a Prison

Had I really thought that this trip would be boring? I was seriously wondering if I would survive to write anything for the competition as I was being thrown around the back of Maddy's ancient banger. (She calls it Monsieur Tacot—that's French for old crock.)

Maddy had waltzed into the hotel lounge as we were all having afternoon tea and celebrating the success of the rally. After Gran and I escaped, it got wilder. When the policeman realised that Dan was faking he tried to arrest him and the Commission building had to be closed while demonstrators shouted and swarmed about. Six wheelchairs blocked off the doors and a man from Marseilles produced a packet of stink-bombs.

There was a lot of hooting and laughing in the lounge. It was worse than class break on a wet morning. I sat munching a *petit pain au chocolat*—(the nearest I could get

to choc-spread sandwiches) — and watching them swap-
ping stories. They were red-faced, excited and mischievous
looking. Dan was mimicking the angry policeman and
Peggy was pretending to be a pin-stripe suit as she swigged
a gin and tonic. The waiters who were ferrying trays of tea
about looked bewildered, especially when Peggy used one
of them to demonstrate how she'd fended off a security
guard with her banner. Bert suddenly got me out of my seat
and called for a round of applause. "A great wee girl she is,"
he shouted. "Stood up for her gran, no nonsense!" There
was clapping. Old ladies tried to kiss me. My neck burned up
and some *petit pain* got stuck in my throat.

As I was choking and rubbing my streaming eyes, Gran
yelped and jumped out of her chair. She wrapped her arms
around a tiny old woman saying, "Maddy, Maddy!" It was
Madeleine Leconte, Gran's old pal, dressed in a moth-eaten
fur coat and high-heeled patent-leather shoes. She had dyed
black hair, bright-red lipstick and a hacking cough that out-
barked Gran's, even on her worst mornings. She kissed Gran
loudly, leaving red lip-prints on her cheek, and then flung
herself into a chair, kicking her legs up and showing a
glimpse of garter. She fluffed her hair out and looked round
at her audience. Flaky stuff swirled around her every time
she moved. I thought she had a bad case of dandruff but
then I realised that bits of her face powder were falling off
and floating like little parachutes.

"Who iz this 'andsome man?" she asked, tapping Bert
on the sleeve. "Nora, you did not tell me you 'ad such
interesting friends!"

Bert blushed and cleared his throat, while Gran shook

her head at Madeleine.

"Stop it, Maddy," she said. "You haven't changed a bit!"

After more tea and sandwiches had been brought, the excitement died down a bit. Maddy covered the carpet with face-flakes while moving her chair closer to Bert's. She fiddled with one of her false eyelashes and told Gran that Philippe was living in a home for old people just outside Brussels.

"I found 'im two weeks ago," she said, "when I was bringing my register of pensioners up to date. A woman who lives in ze block of flats where he 'ad an apartment told me about an old man who 'ad moved out to a home in the country. When I heard 'iz name I was amazed, I couldn't believe it might be the same Philippe. I called at ze home and told 'im you would be here. He was so excited! It iz fate," she pronounced, looking round with a challenging air. "Your fate 'az drawn you together."

Gran was biting her lip. "But is he ill, then?" she asked. "Is he so frail he's had to go into a home?"

I went and sat on the edge of her chair and leaned against her arm. She smelt like Gran should: spicy and herby.

"No, not really," Maddy said vaguely. "He 'az 'ad a pain in 'iz 'art that left 'im weak. He 'az to use a stick." She took out a mirror and repainted her lips with red goo. Bert couldn't take his eyes off her.

"He doesn't need to be in a home if that's all that's wrong with him," said Gran.

Maddy shrugged. "That iz all I know, chérie."

Bumping around in the back of Monsieur Tacot, I began to wish that I hadn't persuaded Gran to bring me along. "You can't drag me all this way," I'd pleaded, "and leave me alone in a strange place while you go off and see your boyfriend. It's not responsible—anything could happen to me!" I was determined not to be left out of the action. It seemed to me that there was something odd about Philippe being in this home. Maddy had looked shifty, as if she wasn't telling all.

I could see that Gran was biting her nails. She was sitting next to Maddy in the passenger seat, hanging on to the dashboard with one hand as the car whooshed round a sharp corner. I leaned forward and tidied up the back of her hair.

"Stop chewing your nails," I told her. "Have you taken your Rescue Remedy?"

She nodded and patted my hand. Her fingers were cold and trembly.

"It'll be all right," I said bravely. That's if we ever get there in one piece, I thought, as Maddy just managed to avoid a truck. In the hotel I'd thought she looked like a hamster who'd seen better days but now she was like a demented gorilla, bent over the wheel in her huge fur coat and fighting with the gears. Strange noises sounded from the car every time she touched the accelerator: whirrs and groans and clanks, as if bits were dropping on to the road.

Gran insisted that I wait in the car while she and Maddy went into the house "to do a reccy." It was a big place with trees standing like sentries at the sides of a long drive. Dark curtains shrouded the windows. I fiddled with the radio but all I could get were moans and whistles and bursts of accordion music. It was such an ancient contraption, it could have been a steam wireless. Then I slipped my tin whistle from my pocket and played it softly—I was on to "Frère Jacques" by now—but I couldn't concentrate. I counted the trees: fifteen. I squeezed my eyes to make the porch lights dance and practised my French conversation. "*Comment allez-vous?*" "*Tres bien, merci.*" What would I say to Philippe? "*Bonsoir, je m'appelle Clare. Ça va?*" It seemed a bit tame but I didn't know how to say: "So, you were once the boyfriend of my grandmother?

I was just about to get out and stretch my legs, when the front door opened and I saw Gran in the porch light. She was waving me in. I ran over and into a hallway that was full of heavy oil-paintings. Gran's voice was hoarse, as if she had a cold.

"Clare," she said, "this is Philippe."

A very thin man held out his hand to me. He looked as if a strong wind would blow him away but his handshake was firm and his skin warm and dry. (Gran says that you can tell a lot about someone by their handshake. Damp, flabby hands spell trouble.) I looked up at bright green eyes. He had a tired face and I liked the way his mouth crinkled.

"You have your grandmother's smile," Philippe said very softly, in perfect English. "I'm delighted to meet you."

He spoke as if the words were an effort and I heard his breath playing a tune in the back of his throat. I was suddenly terrified that he might be ill or about to die and I thought of how unfair it would be on him and Gran. She'd waited so long, hoping that one day he'd turn up. What would she do if he pegged out before they'd even had a chance to talk about the old times? I gave him a good looking-over, trying to decide if he was just very old or very old and on his last legs. He looked back at me and winked.

"Will I do?" he asked.

I felt embarrassed and wished I'd put clean socks on. I looked around at the paintings and polished wood and plush furniture. "This place is dead grand," I said. "It must be really nice living here."

"Appearances can be deceptive," Philippe said, glancing at Gran.

"They certainly can. Never judge a book by its cover, eh?" Gran waved at the walls. "The richer the show, the poorer the spirit. All that glisters is not gold."

I wasn't sure what she was on about. I thought that I wouldn't mind living in a place like this. The deep-pile carpet certainly beat Dad's sale-price, end-of-remnant floor covering.

"The Gestapo couldn't hold you, my dear, and neither will this dreadful house. You have my word. There's more than one kind of enemy to freedom." Gran's voice was fiery.

I could tell that she was nervous because she was moving from one foot to another. Philippe put his hand on her shoulder and nodded at the door.

"You had better go now," he said, "or there will be problems." He didn't sound as if he wanted her to go at all. Gran put her hand on his and shook her head fiercely.

"Too late!" Maddy hissed from the doorway.

A woman hurried into the hall. She had a dark-blue apron and those thin lips that look as if they're saving up nasty words. She stood in front of Philippe and started talking fast in an angry voice. I couldn't understand much of it but it sounded spiteful and bossy. Philippe looked down at the floor and twisted the top of his stick.

"Excuse me!" Gran said loudly, prodding the woman's arm. The woman ignored her and carried on ranting. Maddy hurried over and pushed herself between Philippe and Bossy-Boots. She let fly a burst of French and did a lot of hand-waving. More powder floated and her right eyelash fell to the floor. I picked it up quickly and pocketed it. Philippe had started coughing and holding his chest.

Maddy swung round to Gran. "This woman iz a disgrace," she said. "She should not be allowed to look after people! She says we 'ave no right to be 'ere and we 'ave broken ze rules. Now she insists that we leave. I 'ave told her that she iz a very stupid person and that we are not fooled by her expensive carpets!"

Gran took Philippe's hand anxiously. "I don't want to leave you here," she whispered, "I'm going to get you out."

He nodded and kissed her fingers. "I have dreamed of this," he said, "but I thought that was all it could ever be— a dream. Go now." He coughed hollowly. "You can do nothing more tonight. Look as if you're saying goodbye for good."

Gran threw her arms round him. I hoped she wouldn't hug him too hard; he looked as if he might snap.

"Tomorrow," I heard her whisper, "I'll be back tomorrow."

Bossy-Boots stood by the door with her hands on her hips, shushing us out. I looked back as we went to the car.

Philippe was weaving around on his stick and coughing again but I was sure that he smiled as the door slammed.

Maddy roared up the road and flung the car into a farm gateway. When we'd picked ourselves up, Gran rooted in her bag.

"My God," she said, "I need a cigar." She lit one for Maddy as well and they sat puffing in the front while I spluttered and opened a cracked window.

"What's going on in that place?" I asked. "Why was that woman so mad?" I hadn't liked the look of her at all— she'd had a bunch of keys hanging from her waist, like a gaoler. They'd clanked and clashed as she spoke.

"Philippe is a prisoner," Gran said dramatically. "He's been kept in that place against his will for over a year."

"A prisoner? What did he do? Rob a bank?" He didn't look as if he'd have the strength to carry out a crime.

"No, no." Gran shook her head. "Not that kind of prisoner. Hang on while I get my breath."

She sucked in a bit more cigar poison and then explained what had happened. Philippe had never married and the only family he had left was a niece. When he'd been in hospital after a heart attack his niece had persuaded him to go into Bossy-Boots's home for a rest. Once he was there and still feeling very weak, she'd persuaded him to write a letter to his bank authorising her to cash cheques from his account. She'd said that she'd do up his flat for him if she had some money, but instead she drew out a lot of his savings and vanished.

"That woman, the matron or whatever she calls herself," Gran said angrily, "she knew what the niece was up to.

I expect she got paid a handsome sum to keep quiet."

"It's against the law to kidnap people!" I said. "Couldn't he have told the police?"

"What could he do?" Maddy said. "He iz weak and ill. That woman won't even let 'im near ze phone."

Gran rubbed her forehead. "He's had no one to speak up for him. The niece told people he'd decided to stay there because he liked it so much. Poor Philippe, he thought he'd be stuck there for the rest of his days. Well, he won't be! That woman will keep him there over my dead body!"

"It won't be easy to get 'im out," Maddy said thought-fully. "There iz an alarm system and guard dogs. I heard zem barking."

"We'll find a way," Gran declared. "You should have seen his room, Clare. It's cold and bare, not a bit like the grand hallway. That's just to con visitors. He was hungry, too—he doesn't get enough to eat."

On the way back they told me how they'd managed to get up to Philippe's room on the first floor when the matron wasn't looking. She hadn't wanted to let them in at all. Philippe had been over the moon when he saw Gran. She said that he cried and I thought of his cough and his wobbly legs and that horrible woman not giving him enough to eat and I wanted to go straight back and rescue him.

Philippe a prisoner! I said to myself, watching the lights of Brussels appear. I thought that kind of thing only happened in books, like *The Man In The Iron Mask* or *Escape From Alcatraz*. Was Gran planning to dig a tunnel or lead a midnight raid? What would we do once we got him out? My heart beat fast; I saw myself dressed in black, scaling walls and leaping balconies. Nuala Dunne could have Zermatt. This was a real adventure!

5

More Plots and Plans

Picture the nerve-racking scene: a smoke-filled bed-room in the Hotel Orlando. (Would my lungs survive this journey?) Present are the conspirators, who have gathered to form a daring escape plan: Gran, Maddy, me, Bert, Dan and Peggy. My brain is dancing with wooden horses, helicopters and Star-Trek-type beam-up machines, none of which are much use to Philippe.

Bert keeps saying, "Excuse me, ladies," every time he swears. Gran's description of Philippe's life with Bossy-Boots has got him furious and he's been saying some of those words that are usually shown in comics by @*!@*! marks. Even Peggy's angry. "To think," she says, "that an old person can be locked up like that! It's disgusting. There's no question about it, we must get him out!"

"Yes," Dan growls, "it could have happened to any one of us if we got ill. Taking advantage of an old man's sickness!

I'd like to tear her liver out!"

"And feed it to ze wild animals," Maddy adds grimly.

"And have her guts for garters," I say, not to be left out.

Gran has called the emergency meeting. It will take all of us, she says, to "spring" Philippe. She managed to gather quite a bit of information during her time in the house. There are two guard dogs and an alarm that operates when anyone tries to leave the building. ("She's not worried about anyone trying to break in," Gran snorts, "just people escaping.") There are two other old people living there but they never leave their rooms. Philippe has only glimpsed one of them, a woman who's lost her memory.

"Imagine it," Gran says. "It's like being kept in a cage. Philippe is allowed twenty minutes outside each day, in the tiny back garden. She takes his stick away so that he can't walk far and all the gates are locked while he's there. He spends the rest of the time in his shoe-box of a room. If she's in a good mood he gets a paper to read. He said..." She rubs at her eyes. "He said that he watches the birds flying free and wishes that he could die. He had come to believe that that was the only freedom left."

We're all quiet for a minute but it's a grim silence and you can tell that we're all longing to get that woman and lock *her* up instead.

"Such wickedness!" says Peggy. "It's almost unbelievable!"

"You'd better believe it," Maddy tells her. "But we will avenge 'im!"

Gran calls us to order. "Yes, come on, enough talk; that won't help Philippe. Let's get a strategy worked out."

I've volunteered to take notes of the plan. So far all I've got, underlined three times, is Operation Philippe. The scene now goes something like this:

Gran: (*pacing up and down, puffing a cigar and flicking ash*) That matron's the main problem. We've got to get her out of the way long enough to help Philippe from the house and reach the car.

Maddy: (snorting as she fixes her eyelash back on, spitting on it to help it stick.) That's just ze first problem, chérie. What about ze dogs?

Bert: (*staring gooey-eyed at Maddy*) Steaks. We'll buy big juicy steaks, plenty to keep them busy. Who likes dogs enough to do the feeding?

Short silence

Maddy: OK, I don't mind animals. I'll do that.

Peggy: (*looking puzzled*) If you don't mind me asking, Nora, once you've got Philippe out, what are you going to do with him?

[I've been wondering about this myself.]

Gran: (*flinging her arms wide, French-fashion*) Do with him? I'm taking him back to Ireland, of course! He needs looking after and building up. You don't think I'd leave him here, all alone, almost penniless?

Another short silence

[Gosh, I think, I'll have a grandad! I'd heard of people going to the Continent to shop at the hypermarket but I'd never imagined that you could come back with a brand new grandfather!]

Dan: (*scratching his head*) He's not booked on our party ticket for the ferry. How will we get him on board?

Gran: (*looking withering*) The trouble with you, Dan, is that you lack imagination. Where's the best place to hide a bean? In a can of beans. Where's the best place to hide an old man?

Me: In a group of old people!

Gran: Well done, Clare! You're a chip off the old block!

Bert: What about a passport? He'll need one of those.

Gran: He doesn't have an up-to-date one. We haven't got time to bother with it; we'll just have to brazen it out.

Conspirators look at each other, practising brazen expressions.

The plotting continues, the smoke grows thicker, voices hoarser. Bert's keen on a plan in which one of us rings Bossy-Boots from the hotel and lures her from her house while the others go in and free Philippe but Gran says that too many things could go wrong.

"But we can say that her father's dying!" Bert protests.

"What if her father's already dead?" Gran points out. "We'd feel daft then, wouldn't we?"

Peggy suggests a dawn raid with smoke bombs, fake guns and hoods—I think she's been watching too much television—but this is turned down as being too complicated.

"Where do you think we'll find smoke bombs, Peggy?" Gran asks sarcastically. "Oh yes, there's a shop: 'Ten smoke-bombs, please, and a couple of pretend Lugers!' We wouldn't exactly draw attention to ourselves, would we?"

Dan suggests that he could pretend to be from the Brussels gas board and decoy Bossy-Boots into the kitchen on the pretext of examining her cooker but this is pooh-poohed because a) his French is terrible and b) we don't know if she's got gas.

It's amazing how difficult it is to think clearly when you have to and time's running out; it's like trying to make up an excuse on the spot for not having done your home-work. Finally, at three a.m., after heated arguments, a couple of sulks from Bert and three orders of coffee, I have a completed plan which I read to the exhausted group.

Operation Philippe
Date: 12 April
Estimated time of arrival at prison: 9 p.m./21.00 hours.
Schedule
21.00 hours: Arrive at prison. Park car under trees outside gate. Maddy, Gran and Clare hide by hedge in prison drive. Bert and Dan wait in car (without arguing).
21.05: Peggy knocks on prison door and says that Dan's had a heart attack. Gets Bossy-Boots to accom-pany her to car and keeps her there for ten minutes. (Dan to put on convincing act.)
21.07: Maddy gives steak to dogs. Clare cuts alarm wires.

21.10-21.15: Gran and Clare get Philippe out of prison and hide by hedge. Joined by Bert in case Philippe needs fireman's lift.
21.15: Bossy-Boots returns to house to phone for ambulance. All dash for car and speed away.

"Hang on," Bert says when I've finished. "What if the guard dogs bark before Maddy gets the meat to them, while you're hiding by the hedge?"

"We can't have everything perfect," Gran croaks, taking some foxglove tablets for her throat, "there's got to be some risks. I hope we'll be far enough away from them—it's a long driveway."

"What if Bossy-Boots won't come out of the house?" asks Peggy. "If she's as horrible as you say, she'd probably be happy to let Dan die of a heart attack in the car!"

Gran grits her teeth. "You just have to make sure you get her out, Peggy. Be persuasive!"

"Offer her money if she's not keen," I suggest. "She seems to like money."

"Yes," says Maddy scornfully, "she iz the type who would sell her own mother for thirty pieces of silver. We should show her no mercy; we should deal with her like the Resistance used to deal with traitors…"

"Yes, yes," Gran interrupts, casting her eyes to heaven and rubbing her brow. "Never mind all that, Maddy; that's all long ago. We're a bunch of older citizens and one child; there won't be any violence!"

There's something that's been bothering me as I sit listening to them. The fact that my brain's slowing down doesn't help. My eyes feel as if they've been in a sandstorm.

I check the plan; oh yes, that's it!

"Ahem," I say. "Just a small point: but what do I cut the alarm with?"

I've been selected as wire-cutter because I'm the nimblest and quickest but I'm not sure that I've got the experience for the job. I once helped Dad rescue his car keys by dangling a coat hanger through the driver's window and hooking the keyring but that was in broad daylight and it took twenty minutes.

"Pliers," says Gran. " We can get some in the morning—I mean *this* morning. It'll be dead easy, Clare; just a snip. The alarm box is right by the front door."

She makes it sound so simple. Why aren't I convinced? Dan's been reading the plan again over my shoulder and he clasps his hand to his head. "We've overlooked the most obvious thing," he says. "The car: she'll recognise it from your last visit. We'll have to get another."

"I drive only Monsieur Tacot," Maddy declares irritably. "'E 'az 'iz faults but I know 'im well."

"Dan's right," I say, relieved at the thought of escaping from her old junkheap. "The whole plan will fall apart as soon as she sees Monsieur T." Not to mention the fact, I say to myself darkly, that she'd hear him coming five miles away.

"And we do need a reliable and bigger car for us all," Gran agrees.

"Are you saying that Monsieur Tacot would let us down, Nora?" Maddy bristles, raising her shoulders and sending out a flurry of powder scraps.

"No, not at all," Gran says hastily. "He's...quite an exceptional little car, a complete original. But Dan and

Clare are right: there's no point in going to all this trouble and have her rumble us as soon as we get to the house."

"Very well," Maddy says, still a little wounded, "I will hire a car for the trip. Now, I 'ave so much to do—cars, steak for dogs. I must go to my bed."

The others go off to their rooms, groaning and stretching. I manage to catch Maddy by the door.

"What did the Resistance do?" I whisper. "What did they do to traitors?"

Maddy looks at me silently for a moment. Then she raises her right hand and wordlessly makes a slicing motion across her throat before disappearing into the night.

In bed I close my eyes and curl up on my side, listening to Gran's light snores. I'm exhausted but I can't sleep. I keep seeing dogs with snapping jaws and hearing alarm bells. What if I get it wrong? What if I set the alarm off by mistake, like the time I accidentally switched on the electric ring at school and set fire to the cooking-oil? My hands are sweaty beneath the sheets and my heart is racing. Skiing must be easier than this, I think, at least you can only crunch bones or get sunburned. I could end up in jail; we all could. "Schoolgirl Imprisoned for Attempted Breaking and Entering!"; "European Unity Suffers Blow!"; "Deportation of Law-Breakers!" The newspaper headlines dance in front of my eyes.

Finally I drift into a restless, dream-filled sleep. Miss Casey, dressed as a judge, looks sternly down from a bench and wags her finger. The policeman from the Commission building is tying chains around my ankles while Bert squirts tomato ketchup on his head.

***

6

Operation Philippe

I hadn't read any of my books. They were still stacked on the bedside table. The curse of the Pharaoh's tomb would have to wait a bit longer. I was supposed to have finished *Z For Zacariah* by the start of the new term. My exercise books were untouched by pen. I had more important fish to fry....

It was just as well that my change of clothes consisted of black stretch trousers and a grey sweatshirt. An ideal outfit for a spot of breaking and entering, teamed with plimsolls for speed. Pity I hadn't brought a balaclava. Gran was obviously on the same wavelength because she came out of the bathroom wearing the quietest garment she possesses, a navy-blue tracksuit. We looked each other up and down.

"Nervous?" she asked.

"A bit. I bet Dad wouldn't have been so keen for me to

come if he'd known you were going to involve me in daring deeds!"

"What he doesn't know won't worry him," Gran said smugly. "Now come and take some distilled rosemary. It'll quieten your jitters."

I took the tablets and sucked them. "I wonder what Philippe's been doing during all the years since the war?" I wondered aloud. "Did you ask him?"

"We haven't had much time to catch up," Gran said. "He's managed to tell me a little bit; he was very ill after the war, had a long spell in hospital. He tried to trace me in the 'fifties but couldn't find me. I'd moved around, of course, and he didn't know my married name. He took a teaching job and paid for his niece to go to college."

"What, the one who stashed him away in that home?"

"The very one. It just goes to show: your nearest and dearest can turn on you."

"What a worm! He must really hate her."

"I shouldn't think so, knowing the Philippe of old. He probably curses himself for having been taken in but he wouldn't hate."

"Not even the Germans? Didn't he hate them?"

"No. He despised the leaders and their evil but he never hated the ordinary Germans who were cannon-fodder. You can't hate a whole people: it doesn't make sense."

"Bert and Dan seem to. They treat each other like enemies."

Gran laughed. "They don't truly hate: they just can't let go of old wounds. They're both lonely so they look for someone or something to pick a fight with. They've got more in common than they think."

I decided to mull that over. "Gran," I said slowly, watching her from the corner of my eye, "did you want me to come on this trip so that I could meet Philippe?"

"Oh, well, you know," she said airily, fiddling with the lace of her sneaker, "I thought that if Maddy found him—and I was only hopeful before we left—that it would be a good opportunity for you to see him. He means such a lot to me, you see, and so do you. Of course, I'd no idea that we'd have to spring him from that terrible place." She straightened up, a bit flushed. "Now, have you had enough practice with those cutters?"

"I think so. My wrist's aching."

Gran had bought me some nasty-looking pliers and a short length of electric cable so that I could get familiar with my job. I'd spent the afternoon snipping off bits of cable, timing myself; I could get from the door of the bedroom to the wire and cut through a section in two minutes.

"Right," she said, looking at her watch. "It's nearly eight. Let's run a check before we go down and meet the others."

We moved over to the small table and went through our collection of goodies for Operation Philippe.

"Steak," called Gran.

"Check!" There were five huge pieces, bloody and fat, enough to keep the wildest dogs busy for a while.

"Pliers."

"Check!"

"Clothes for Philippe."

"Check!" We'd sent Bert to buy him an outfit. They were about the same height, although Philippe was much thinner. Bert had come back with a stripy shirt and brown crimplene trousers. Crimplene! Yuk! Gran had ignored Bert's awful taste, saying that they'd do Philippe until we got him back to Newcastle. (We couldn't bank on taking any clothes from the prison. He'd told Gran that Bossy-Boots kept his things locked away. That made me feel peculiar and shivery.)

There was something fluttering in my stomach. The palms of my hands were cold and clammy. My late-night plotting was catching up with me. The excitement of preparation was dying away. What am I doing messing about with all this? I thought, feeling cowardly. I looked at the pliers, witness to my forthcoming criminal activity, and I wanted to be at home, snuggled up on my bed with my Walkman plugged in. Even a bit of meditation in Donegal would be preferable.

"I suppose," I said feebly, as Gran swept the steak and pliers into a rucksack, "we could be in big trouble if it goes wrong tonight."

Gran looked at me, her head on one side. "I know I'm asking a lot of you," she said, "but I wouldn't ask if I didn't think you could do it." She came and sat beside me. "We're not doing anything really wrong, you know. Cutting the cable's a bit naughty but that's easily mended. Philippe is a prisoner there and he has a right to his liberty. You wouldn't want to go back to Ireland knowing that he's in that woman's clutches, would you?"

I shook my head, wishing that I could be braver.

"It'll all be fine," Gran said, rubbing my shoulder. "Nothing can go wrong. We've a good plan and our cause is just! We'll have him in Ireland before we know it. It's a night you'll always remember—the night we rescued Philippe!"

On the way down in the lift I kept repeating to myself, "Our cause is just! Our cause is just!" It made me feel better; I strode across the foyer like a musketeer going into battle. One for all and all for one! Gran looked determined as she led the way out to the others, who were waiting by the side of the hotel.

Our four fellow-conspirators were standing beside a gleaming estate car. Peggy, Dan and Bert were wearing identical trousers and polo-necks. I thought that Bert must have bought them while he was out shopping and I imagined him asking for help in a store; "Ah, can you recommend anything smart but comfy for a guerilla-type night raid? Not too pricey, you understand." I gaped at Maddy. Her face was scrubbed of make-up, her hair shoved under a black beret. She was wearing khaki drill trousers and a belted camouflage jacket. As we came up she saluted briskly. She looked like a completely different person; not a hamster or a gorilla but a sleek, alert leopard.

Bert stood to attention. His face was lit up. "All present and correct," he said eagerly. "It's good to be back in harness."

"Where's your walking-stick?" I asked Peggy.

She laughed. "I don't need it tonight. I feel about twenty-five!"

Gran cast her eye over Maddy. "You don't think the

outfit's a tiny bit over the top?" she asked drily.

"I am ready for action," Maddy declared, "primed and fit. Now, into the car. *Allons!*"

We piled in, Gran and Maddy in the front; me, Bert, Peggy and Dan in the back. Gran issued a stern warning to Dan and Bert: "We all know you two don't see eye to eye but I don't want any arguing on this mission, understand? We're all united in the cause!"

Dan pulled his collar up. "Dev never found me wanting," he said stoutly, "and neither will you, Nora. I haven't forgotten my training in the Wicklow mountains," he added proudly, giving Bert a sly sideways glance.

"Parade-ground discipline," promised Bert. "No back-chat to the commander."

Gran nodded. "Glad to hear it. Let's just check one last time that we all know what we're doing."

We ran through the plan before Maddy started the car. I'd had a last-minute idea. I took my whistle out and gave it to Dan.

"If anything goes wrong while we're in the house," I told him, "blow hard on that to warn us."

"Good thinking," he said, blasting a shrill note that gave us earache.

Gran made us all take a dose of rosemary and wild honeysuckle and we set off. You could feel the tension and excitement. Gran kept playing with the zip of the rucksack. Dan gave us brief snatches of whistle tunes. (I identified "The Battle Of Jericho" and "The Minstrel Boy.") Peggy sang "The Peeler And The Goat" and Bert wound a shred of his moustache round and round his finger. I chewed at the inside of my mouth even though I knew it would give me horrible ulcers.

"Ah," said Dan, "this reminds me of night-training and manœuvres. We'd creep through villages, staying out of the moonlight. There's many a cat got a fright when it saw us."

Bert laughed. "Cats!" he said. "It was the Jerries we frightened. Hand-to-hand combat, that was the name of our game. Proper soldiers, we were, highly trained machines."

Gran made a warning noise in her throat and Maddy chuckled. She seemed to be thoroughly enjoying herself. She sat back in the driver's seat, puffing away and tapping her long fingernails in time to the music.

"Joshua fit ze battle of Jericho and ze walls came tumbe-ling down," she sang, bringing her fist down on the driving wheel and cackling. "You men in ze back," she said, "you must not be ze prisoners of your pasts. That is not ze way forward. Now you are on ze same side, ze side of humanity. You fight for your own kind. Age, it knows no barriers, eh?"

"Suppose so," said Bert quietly.

Dan nodded. "You've a point there."

Maddy's beret had slipped to one side and was dangling wildly over her left eye. It gave her a daring, rakish look, especially as tufts of her hair were sticking out below its rim. I chewed faster at my mouth.

"Were you ever injured?" I heard Bert ask Dan.

"In the leg. I've a scar."

I knew from Gran that Dan had acquired his scar

during a collision with a milk-churn in Bray but I didn't say anything. I was too busy wondering about Maddy's intimate knowledge of the Resistance. I heard her laugh and say to Gran, "Ah, chérie, I 'aven't felt so alive for years! This is like ze old days, a cause to fight for, a battle to win!"

"Just keep your eyes on the road," Gran said, "and never mind the flights of fancy. We all know the risks you took in the past."

I didn't like the sound of that. What risks? I sat back, watching the flat countryside, imagining what my friends would be doing tonight; watching TV, going to the cinema, listening to tapes. Nuala Dunne would be at the *après-ski* club in one of the outfits she'd bought with the hundred pounds her dad had given her for holiday gear. An unreal, spooky sensation started to creep through me. I blinked, thinking that I might wake up and find that this had all been a dream. What was a fourteen-year-old doing with a crazy old Resistance fighter, three pounds of dripping steak and a pair of pliers? Surely this wasn't what Miss Casey had intended for her talented pupil? Stop the car! I wanted to shout, I've changed my mind!

Gran turned to us. "Soon he'll be safe with us," she said. "Free at last. Dear Philippe. One of the bravest people I've known."

I sat forward, flexing my hand. "Give me those pliers, Gran," I said, "I want to get some more practice."

Let's just say that even the best plan has to have one or two flaws. At first all went smoothly, just as we'd organised. Gran, Maddy and I hid behind a huge beech tree while Dan practised his choking sounds and Peggy hurried up to the prison door.

"The weather iz with us," Maddy whispered from behind a low branch. "Some cloud cover but light enough to see ze way. We used to pray for such nights so that ze Boche wouldn't see us."

"Who were the Boche?" I asked.

"The Germans. A cloudy night made it easier to travel."

"Travel where?"

"On operations, across country. Now ssh! Peggy's ringing ze bell."

I thought of Maddy flitting through dark nights, hiding from the enemy. She wouldn't have worn face-powder then—it would have left a tell-tale trail. It seemed to me, standing under the whispering leaves, that Gran was turning out to have very mysterious friends indeed.

The door was opened. We could hear Peggy talking in a high voice and see her pointing back down the driveway.

"She's putting on an brilliant act," I said admiringly.

"She used to be in amateur dramatics," Gran whispered. "Her best roles were Souhaun in *Purple Dust* and Lady Macbeth."

Peggy's antics did the trick. Bossy-Boots came out the door with Peggy tugging at her arm and, most importantly, left the door open in her hurry. (We'd been counting on that—don't ask what we'd have done if she'd shut it.) I waited until they'd disappeared through the tall gates and then set off, speeding for the door. Maddy and Gran raced along beside me; Maddy veered off to the left, heading for the kennel at the side of the house. Now that it was actually happening, I felt great, not a bit scared. My blood was pumping and I thought I could do anything in the world. The moon peeped out from behind a cloud, long enough to show me the small red alarm box fitted to the wall and the wires that ran by a climbing ivy. Standing on tiptoe, I placed the pliers close to the box and snipped as hard as I could. It was so easy I was taken aback, and for a few seconds I just stood there, amazed that I'd actually done it.

"Come on, come on," Gran hissed. "No time to waste."

She led the way at a run, diving through the door, along a corridor and up a flight of steep wooden stairs. "This way!" she panted, turning to her right and dashing to the end of the passageway. She threw a door open and there was Philippe, sitting in pyjamas on his bed, looking astonished.

"Nora!" he gasped. "It is you! You have really re-turned!"

"Of course I have," she said, sucking at air. "Now hurry, we have very little time."

It was a tiny room, like a box. The three of us filled it. I glanced around, thinking that this was where Philippe had to spend most of his days. It had peeling wallpaper and one shelf. It looked like a place where you could die of boredom.

He got straight off the bed, swaying, and reached for his stick.

"Have you any shoes or slippers?" Gran asked.

"No. She takes them away in the evening. Don't worry, let's just go. I will need a steadying hand on the stairs."

We made our way back along the passage as quickly as we could. Philippe shuffled, breathing hard. He was grasp-ing his stick so tightly I thought his knuckles would crack.

I went first on the stairs while Gran held his free hand and carried his stick. He leaned heavily on the bannister. Hurry, hurry, hurry, I was saying to myself, looking at my watch. Our ten minutes was nearly up. Peggy wouldn't be able to keep Bossy-Boots away much longer and we still had to get to the hedge at the end of the drive. There was no way that Philippe was going to be able to run. Everything seemed to have gone into slow motion. The air was thick and hard to breathe. Philippe's wheezing reminded me of Monsieur Tacot.

As we got to the bottom of the stairs the phone in the hallway started to ring. A moment later, there was a penetrating blast on the tin whistle. We froze.

"Oh no," Gran moaned. "Quick, or she'll be here!"

I grabbed at Philippe and Gran got him under the elbow but as we were half-way across the hall Bossy-Boots came running through the door and stopped in her tracks. The blasted phone stopped ringing. She looked furious. Her lips went back over her teeth and I half expected to see fangs. She started shouting and waving her fist at Gran, who tried to edge Philippe towards the door. Bossy-Boots stood smartly in front, blocking it. I heard "gendarmes" a couple of times as she ranted and hissed.

"Get out of the way, you horrible old biddy," Gran shouted. She was holding Philippe's stick horizontally in front of her, like an Oriental weapon. "Back!" she shrieked, cutting it through the air.

Bossy-Boots wasn't impressed. She glared at Philippe and moved towards him as if he were the juicy morsel she'd been saving for supper. He started to buckle at the knees and tremble. I tightened my hold on him. His bones felt like twigs. This was it, I was thinking; there was no hope now. Philippe was going to end up on the floor, a fly to her spider, and we'd have to scarper without him.

"I'll use this," Gran was threatening, "I'm warning you, I will," when a small figure leapt on Bossy-Boots from behind and twisted her arm up her back. The two cavorted around the floor, groaning and puffing.

"Go on, Maddy," Gran called. "Show her what you're made of!"

A large, priceless-looking vase full of dried flowers rocked alarmingly as they tumbled into a corner. It smashed into pieces, spraying through the air. Maddy now had both Bossy-Boots's arms secured. She looked like a fierce kitten worrying a huge cat. Her beret was hanging on by one hatpin as Bossy-Boots twisted, trying to throw her off.

"This isn't a show," Maddy shouted at us crossly. "Make for ze car, quickly! Get Philippe in and be ready to go!"

"But will you be all right?" Gran called anxiously as an oil-painting thumped on to the umbrella stand.

"*Mon Dieu*, yes! Don't waste time, idiots!" she yelled crossly, pulling fierce faces.

Gran and I grabbed Philippe, each holding one arm, and headed out the door and down the drive. The gravel cut into his feet and he bit his lip hard. We half-carried, half-dragged him along, ignoring the din that was coming from the house. The last few yards were like eternity. I was praying that we wouldn't drop him before we reached the car.

Peggy, Dan and Bert came running towards us as we left the gates.

"I tried to stop her," Peggy shouted, "but she got suspicious. What's happening?"

"Never mind; just help us to the car," Gran said, draping Philippe's arms round Dan and Bert's shoulders.

I waited until they had him safe and then I slipped away and headed back to the house. If that woman managed to turn the tables on Maddy she'd be able to overpower her. My feet threw gravel into the air as I pounded back, skidding to a halt as Maddy came through the front door.

"Are you okay? Where is she?" I tried to ignore the stitch in my side.

Maddy rubbed her hands and smiled at me. "I 'ave dealt with her," she said nonchalantly. "We will 'ave no more trouble from her."

I stared at her pleased expression and her hands. Her voice echoed back to me from the hotel bedroom; "...like the Resistance used to deal with traitors..." No, I thought...she can't have...she wouldn't...not that!

She turned me round with a little push. "Come," she said, "we must lose no time now," and hurried me to the gates.

I wondered if there were blood on her hands and under her fingernails and if we would be put on trial as—what was it?—accomplices. Would we be jailed in Belgium or would they send us back to Ireland handcuffed together? Would my friends come and see me in prison or would they shudder at the thought of me? My mouth had gone dry and sour-tasting. Maddy was giving little chuckles as she beetled along beside me. They made my spine tingle.

Philippe was in the back of the car with a blanket round him. Bert got into the front with Maddy as she started the engine and pulled out with a screech of tyres. I sank back against Gran's shoulder, wondering how to tell her the dreadful news. She was stroking Philippe's cheek and holding his bony hand in hers.

"Well," she said with a huge sigh, "we've pulled it off, in spite of last-minute difficulties. I really thought we were goners when that woman came back."

"My heart was in my mouth," Peggy said. "Dan put on a good show, plenty of groans and twitches but she insisted on getting back to the house. I managed to keep her a bit longer with a few screams but she was suspicious."

"She won't be kidnapping any more old people," Maddy stated, "she 'az learned that grey power iz not to be messed with!" She tapped a cigarette from a packet. I wished she'd keep both hands on the wheel.

"I cannot believe it," said Philippe faintly, "I cannot believe that I will never have to hear her sharp voice again or eat her thin soup. Her coffee was like that dreadful grey liquid we used to have during the war, tasteless and bitter."

Gran hugged him. "You're safe now," she said. He put his arm round her and kissed her cheek. I looked out of the window. I hate sloppy scenes. It was worse than watching snoggers at the back of the cinema. My heart was in my boots. I wondered how long it would be before the body was found. Was that the wail of a police siren already? I strained my ears but all I could hear was the sound of the wind rushing past the car.

Maddy had her foot pressed down on the accelerator. She didn't seem to have anything on her mind. I half-admired her cool; fancy cutting someone's throat and being so light-hearted! Perhaps her years in the Resistance had hardened her and made her a cold-blooded killer. Gran would have to know, and the sooner the better. I didn't like to interrupt her snog but I had to tell her the awful truth.

I was just about to tap her on the arm when Bert leaned forward and put his hand on Maddy's shoulder.

"What did you do to the woman?" he asked. "Will she be after us soon?"

"Not a chance," said Maddy. "I tied her up and locked her in ze office. I threw ze key into ze shrubbery so that even if someone finds her, it will take a while to release her. I will ring ze police anonymously in ze morning in case she is still zere."

"A night's thought about her crimes will do her good," said Peggy hotly. "She's a terrible woman. She was prodding and poking Dan as if he was a piece of meat."

"I'm sure I've bruises," complained Dan. "She had nails like razors."

"I know." Maddy nodded her head vigorously. "I 'ad a terrible time with her. All my unarmed combat experience was necessary. The knee in the small of ze back finally did ze trick."

I swallowed hard. Thank goodness I hadn't opened my mouth and made a complete fool of myself. I was so relieved that there was no corpse that I started to laugh helplessly. The others stared at me for a moment and then they started too until the car was rocking with chuckles and guffaws. Philippe had a coughing fit but he kept on laughing through it. He flung his arms around Gran, Peggy and me, and squeezed us as tightly as an old man with sparrow-thin arms can.

"Liberty," he cried, "sweet liberty!"

In the front, Bert leaned over and kissed Maddy on the cheek, knocking her beret sideways. She gave him a thump in the ribs that made him gasp, but she laughed at him and blew him a loud kiss through her fingers.

"I'm starving!" Philippe announced. "I could eat a wolf!"

"Do you like *petit pain au chocolat*?" I asked him, searching in my pocket for the pastry I'd hidden at breakfast. It was warm and squashy but it still smelled good.

He took it from me and ate it in one gulp, without chewing. I stared; even *I* couldn't eat them that fast. I reckoned that Philippe might well become an ally in the production of choc-spread sandwich feasts.

***

7

Wine, Song and a Policeman

I'd never had so many late nights. When we got back to the hotel we crept up quietly to Gran's room and mine. So as not to raise any suspicions, Maddy went to a take-away to get Philippe some food and came back with a feast of chicken and pizzas for everyone. Bert cracked open some of the wine he'd bought on the boat and we sat around gorging ourselves. Gran wouldn't let Philippe eat too much, which I thought was unfair, considering that he'd been hungry for so long, but she explained that it might make him ill if he suddenly filled his stomach. He watered his wine down and took small mouthfuls. I think he was dazed at the sight of so much food.

Maddy did have some blood on her right hand but it had been caused by a scratch from a dog, not from cutting someone's throat. One of the dogs had raked her fingers with its teeth as she was giving it steak. Gran bathed it for her and soothed it with marigold ointment.

"A battle scar to be proud of," Bert said, kissing her other hand. I thought that Bert was getting a bit over the top but Maddy seemed to be enjoying the attention. These old people, I thought, downing my third can of fizzy drink; you'd think they'd behave better!

"It is good to 'ave a scar again," Maddy declared, "to feel the passion of the fight, pitting your wits against ze enemy! You remember, Philippe, how we were always ready, always alert for danger?"

"How could I forget?" he said. "I have never had friends like the ones I had then. In the long hours in that house I used to think about you all. I recalled the nights when we led escaped prisoners and carried messages." He looked at me and smiled. "But Clare might not wish to know of these things. It was all so long ago. The old must not bore the young with their memories."

Was he kidding? I was dying to know the whole lot: who'd done what, and when. I was getting pretty fed up with all the mystery.

"Tell me," I said, "tell me about what you did. Did you nearly get killed?"

I couldn't believe the stuff they started to come out with; it was like Indiana Jones, Star Wars and Buck Rogers all mixed together. Philippe had been in charge of an escape line to Switzerland; Maddy had acted as a guide and had also been a courier, taking messages to safe houses and passing on plans.

"Do you remember when the Boche nearly caught you, Maddy?" Philippe asked. "You had to hide under floorboards."

"I thought I'd never walk again," Maddy grinned, "but I didn't sneeze or cough. They weren't going to get me!"

There were tales of midnight raids, people hiding in lofts, trains being blown up and lorries hijacked. Philippe had been captured twice; the first time he managed to escape by jumping a barbed wire fence. Bert revealed that he'd been a member of a special operations squad that infiltrated behind German lines to dynamite key communication lines. My jaw started to drop; I'd started out on a coach trip with a party of old people who had enough tablets to stock a hospital and enough wrinkles between them to carpet Europe from end to end and I'd discovered I was in the middle of ace plotters, secret agents and derring-do guerrilla fighters. What was that song my dad sang sometimes? "Stop The World, I Want To Get Off!"

Philippe raised his glass to Dan and Bert. "I must thank you especially," he said. "Without your broad shoulders I think I would have collapsed in the road. You work as a team, yes? You were comrades in the war?"

I realised that I hadn't heard Bert and Dan arguing for several hours. Gran laughed and planted a kiss first on Dan's cheek, then on Bert's. They sat looking baffled.

"You've rendered them speechless, thank goodness!" she told Philippe. "They can't believe they've worked as a team!"

More wine was poured to save their blushes. Then Gran sang a very rude song about Hitler's anatomy and I whistled "Pack Up Your Troubles In Your Old Kit Bag." (I haven't watched those old war films without learning something.) Dan started the first verse of "Home On The Range" and Bert joined in, drumming on an empty pizza carton. Maddy was sitting on Bert's knee while she and Philippe sang "It's A Long Way To Tipperary." Gran tapped on an empty bottle as an accompaniment.

There was a knock on the door.

"Oh dear," Gran said, "we've probably woken someone up. What's the time?"

"One o'clock," I said. "I bet we've been making a racket."

Maddy did have a very loud contralto; she'd been belting out, "Goodbye Piccadilly, farewell Leicester Square" and waving her glass wildly. (Some of her wine had gone in Bert's ear but he didn't seem to mind.) They were all giggling and pink-faced. Bert had been mixing beer and wine and was crooning something about being a lonesome cowboy while Dan made howling coyote noises. Gran hiccuped and beat at her chest. Philippe was tottering on his chair, about to fall on the carpet any minute.

What a bunch of hooligans, I thought, realising that I'd have to take responsibility. It was just as well they had me with them. Somebody had to stay clear-headed! They all seemed to have forgotten the knock. Maddy was smacking Philippe's knee with a chicken wing.

"Hey," she said, "you remember zat dishy friend you 'ad, Philippe? Ze one wiz ze little beard and curly hair? He 'ad wonderful brown eyes and a voice like honey. What happened to 'im?"

"Marcel? He settled in Lyons after the war and started a carpentry business. He died three years ago. He'd got very fat."

"Oh," Maddy said, "fat men I cannot stand, it iz just az well I forgot 'im."

Bert looked relieved and sat up straight, pulling his tummy in. He'd have to stop wearing tight-fitting polo necks.

The knock came at the door again, more insistent. None of them took any notice.

"Shall I get that?" I asked, not expecting an answer. Now I knew what Miss Casey felt like when she couldn't get us to pay attention.

I went into the little hallway and opened the door. A man in a dark grey suit was standing there. He looked me up and down for a moment and nodded to himself. I didn't like the nod; it seemed to mean that he knew something.

"Can I help you?" I said grandly, keeping the door handle gripped firmly.

"Yes, Mademoiselle, I think you can. I am a police officer. Can I please speak to an adult?"

He spoke very slowly and correctly, as if he was selecting his English words from a dusty dictionary. My knees went wobbly and spots danced in front of my eyes. I opened my mouth but a strangled croak came out.

"There is an adult here?" he asked, trying to peer past me.

I could hardly have denied it. It sounded as if there was a zoo in the bedroom, with the monkeys fighting for bananas. I tried to think.

"A *policeman*?" I said as loudly as I could, half-closing the door and throwing my voice back along the hallway. "*Good heavens, a policeman*? Do you have any identification?" I asked. Gran was always warning old people to check the identity of callers.

He reached into his pocket and brought out a small plastic card with his picture. He pointed with his forefinger. "That is me, Jean Dubois, officer of the Brussels police. Now, may I come in, please?"

I pretended to examine the card closely, aware of a sudden silence and scuffling noises from the bedroom. "Well," I said, "we've not had a *policeman* visit us here before." I tried to sound casual, as if it was normal to hold a conversation with the police at one o'clock in the morning. "Have you visited many other hotels tonight?" I asked.

"No, not tonight," he said patiently.

"It's not a parking ticket, is it?" I asked, stalling for time.

"No," he said, beginning to look restless. "Can you please...?" To my relief, Gran came out, dabbing at her cheeks with a hanky.

"Good evening, ossifer," she said, stifling a burp. "C...can I help you?"

"Perhaps," he said. "I think it would be best if I came in. We do not wish to disturb other guests."

"Certainly," said Gran. She looked at me as if I'd materialised from the woodwork. "Good heavens, Clare!" she exclaimed, "are you still up?"

My mouth hanging open, I trailed after them into the bedroom. Philippe had vanished. Maddy was no longer on Bert's knee but was reclining on Gran's bed with her cheek propped on her hand, the picture of innocence. Dan was holding a ball of wool for Peggy, who had produced knitting-needles and was casting on stitches, her glasses perched on the end of her nose. The effect was a little spoiled by the two empty wine bottles lying at her feet. I saw the policeman take in the empty food cartons, the cigar stubs and the half-filled glasses. He'd have to be pretty dense to believe that we'd been having a cosy knitting-circle in the small hours. I wondered where they'd put Philippe, and decided that he must be hiding in the bathroom. That wouldn't be much good, I thought glumly, if the policeman had a search warrant. Our daring deeds might have been in vain.

"Good evening," Peggy said with a big smile, making her voice doddery. "Does your granny knit, young man?"

"No, she does not. And I think it is good morning, Madame," he said, nodding to her.

"Is that right?" Bert said, eyes wide. "Who'd have thought it could be that late? We were just having a little celebration," he explained. "It's my birthday and Peggy here said she'd knit me a jumper." He spoke almost as slowly as the policeman but he was having to choose his words from the beery fog in his head.

"How kind," the policeman said, sniffing the air.

"It is indeed," Bert agreed. "My old bones play me up something terrible in wet weather. It'll be great to have a warm jumper. I can't get around much these days, you see," he added, trying to look feeble.

"You managed to travel from Ireland?" the policeman asked.

"Ah well, you know, the wonders of modern transport..." Bert coughed and blinked.

"May I sit down?" the policeman asked Gran. "This is your room, Mrs Quarry?"

"Yes and yes," she said, sinking down herself.

The policeman pulled up a chair and placed it facing Maddy and the bathroom. "I will explain why I have come," he said. "Maybe you will be able to help me with an enquiry about a missing gentleman."

"We will if we can," Gran said, holding the sides of her chair as if she expected it to take off, "but I don't think we're missing anyone. Have you missed anyone, Maddy?"

"No, no one." Maddy beamed at the policeman and plumped up a pillow to rest her elbow on.

The policeman fiddled with the knot of his tie. "We have had a report tonight from a Madame Delon," he said. "She rents rooms to old people. Earlier tonight—that is, late last night—she was locked in her house and one of her residents was taken away. She says that several elderly people were involved, that they were Irish and that they had a young, dark-haired girl with them."

I should definitely have bought a wig, I thought. As the policeman paused significantly I saw to my horror that Philippe's ankle was jutting out from beneath Gran's bed. I pulled a face at Maddy and wiggled my eyebrows, nodding downwards. She kept a straight face and said, "Clare, chérie, could you get me my glass? I left it on ze table." I picked up a glass and took it to her, sitting down beside her as she patted the bedspread. As I squirmed around I nudged Philippe's ankle and felt it pull away.

"That's amazing," Gran said, looking the policeman straight in the eye. "I can't imagine such a thing."

"It is rather a coincidence that the people in here fit the description, is it not, Madame?"

"Officer, you're not suggesting that we had anything to do with it?" Peggy looked at him over her knitting with a wounded expression.

"You know nothing about alarm wires being cut, an elderly man being taken from his room and..." The policeman consulted a notebook. "Oh yes, a small woman who used judo to force Madame Delon into a room and told her..." He consulted his notes again."Told her that if she did not stay quiet she would have the treatment that traitors deserve."

Gran gave a light-hearted laugh. "It sounds like something the SAS carried out," she said. "Can you imagine old people and a mere child doing all that? I'd like to know what vitamins they're on!"

I didn't care for the mere child bit. I scowled at Gran but she was too busy looking innocent for the policeman.

"A glass of wine?" she asked him. "Please do, in celebration of Bert's birthday."

"Thank you," he said, to my amazement. I thought policemen were supposed to refuse bribes? He sniffed the wine deeply and then raised the glass to Bert, saying "*Salut!*" After a few appreciative sips he turned to Gran and said, "Could you please explain where you have been tonight?"

There was an awkward silence. The policeman was looking at all of us in turn. I kept getting the impression that he was trying not to laugh. Now, I've read lots of detective stories and I know it's best to stick to the truth as much as possible when you're providing an alibi.

"We went for a drive," I said brightly, "with Maddy. We're only here for a few days, you see, and we wanted to do some sightseeing. It was brilliant."

The policeman looked at me keenly. "I see," he said. "And you all went?"

"Oh yes," Maddy assured him, "it was a bit of a squeeze."

We all nodded, trying to look like interested tourists. Dan had fetched a jug of water and given glasses of it to Gran and Bert. They seemed to be sobering up fast. I watched the policeman and willed him to go soon. I didn't think that lying on the floor would do Philippe much good. Gran kept glancing at the edge of the bed and biting her lip when the policeman turned away from her.

The policeman gave a big sigh and put his glass down. Oh good, I thought, he's going! We weren't about to be taken to the police station after all and questioned under bright spotlights until one of us squealed. He was a kind-looking man but I imagined that he must have handcuffs in his pocket or maybe even a back-up team waiting in the corridor, ready to tackle the judo expert.

"They must be desperate people, these kidnappers," he said. "Brussels will not be safe until we catch them. I hope there is not going to be an epidemic of old people being snatched from their homes. What can their purpose be, do you think? It is too horrible to think about."

We stared at him. Everyone was fully alert.

"Perhaps they had a good reason," Gran said quietly. "Perhaps you don't know the whole story."

The policeman smiled at her. "Perhaps not," he said,

"but I would like to ask, Madame. I do think that the gentleman under the bed should come out now; it is not a good place for old bones."

"Gentleman, what gentleman?" Gran was saying, but Philippe was crawling slowly out and raising himself to a sitting position. Dust flew up around him and Maddy sneezed violently.

"Good morning, Monsieur," the policeman said solemnly. "I am Jean Dubois and I am pleased to meet you."

"Good morning," Philippe said weakly. Maddy and I helped him up and sat him on the edge of the bed. "I have a terrible headache," he said. "Can I have a glass of water?"

Dan fetched him a drink while the rest of us watched in stunned silence. Even Gran seemed lost for words, but only for a moment or two. She went and sat beside Philippe on the bed.

"You're not taking him back there," she said firmly, "never. You can put me in jail, lock me up but you won't let her have Philippe back."

"That iz right." Maddy leapt up, hands on hips, legs apart. "Philippe has friends who won't let 'im be ill-treated again. We do not forget our own and we will deal with anyone who tries to take 'im from us!"

"We'll get all the pensioners down to your police station," Peggy said, her knitting abandoned behind her and a scowl on her face. "We'll make such a fuss you'll beg us to go away."

"I'll get all the schoolchildren in Brussels on strike," I said wildly.

Bert started to march up and down, saluting. "Comrades don't forget old comrades!" he barked. "Our bones might be old but our hearts are young and strong!" Dan joined him, in step, arms swinging; "Ourselves alone! We will fight on the streets, we will fight..."

"Please, please!" The policeman was laughing and holding his hands to his ears. "You will not need to do all these things, I assure you!"

"You mean you're not going to arrest us?" I asked hopefully.

"No, I am not. I think you are not such desperate criminals after all."

"No, they are not. They are the best friends a man can ever hope to have." Philippe had been sitting quietly, exhausted and aching from his cramped hiding-place. He sat up straight. "If you must take me back, then you will have to, but nothing must happen to these good people who have risked everything for me."

"No!"

"Over our dead bodies!"

"Just you try!"

"Not a chance!"

"*Vive la Résistance et la liberté!*"

We all shouted at once. The policeman flinched, holding up his hands.

"I think I understand what you are telling me," he said. "Please, sit down all of you before the hotel manager arrives and we are all in trouble."

We sank back into our seats and watched him suspiciously. Maddy looked as if she was ready to do a triple-action armlock on him if he made a wrong move.

"Permit me to tell you a story," he said, pouring himself another glass of wine and loosening his tie. "A year ago a man took his elderly mother to look at some nursing homes. In the course of his enquiries he came across a house just outside the city run by a Madame Delon. He did not like the woman and the atmosphere in her house. In the nearby village he heard people report that this woman was very unpleasant. The old people she looked after were never seen. The shopkeepers said that she ordered little food. There have been stories about her since then, nasty tales but no evidence. The police have been keeping an eye on her but they needed proof of what they suspected was happening there. Now, perhaps, they have it."

"You were the man!" I said. "It was your mother."

He nodded at me. "Well done; you have guessed correctly."

"So you wouldn't want to send Philippe back?" Gran said excitedly.

"Of course not! You think I am a bully? It would be over *my* dead body, Madame. When this woman telephoned us I was beside myself. I was so much hoping that I would find you so that we would have real evidence to prosecute her!"

"Well," said Gran with a huge sigh, "more wine, anyone?"

Glasses were filled and raised.

"*Salut* again!" said the policeman.

"You're not worried about the alarm and the steak and the judo?" I asked him, just to make sure.

"What alarm, what steak, what judo?" he said, shrugging. "I have not heard of these things. Did you dream them?"

I was half-convinced that I had. It seemed years ago since I'd reached up and snipped with the pliers. I drank a glass of wine—nobody seemed bothered that it might be the start of an alcoholic career—and listened as Philippe told the policeman about the prison. I had a second glass to keep the first company. Maddy started to sing again, a song about fighting and being true to the cause and the policeman joined in the chorus. He'd taken off his jacket and was sitting cross-legged on the floor with one of Gran's cigars stuck between his teeth.

I snuggled down and rested my head against Maddy's arm, thinking in a drowsy way that Nuala Dunne might have found the romance she'd been planning with a ski instructor. Squinting at them through the smoke, at Bert and Peggy dancing in the middle of the floor, Dan and Gran playing the spoons and the policeman and Philippe clapping, I yawned and thought that there was nowhere else I'd rather be.

***

8

Hangovers and (More) Heart Attacks

I would never again hit the wine bottle. Not for me the career of a teenage drinker! My head wanted to stay on the pillow and let the rest of my body walk around. No, that's not the truth. My legs and stomach would have liked to be horizontal, too. (They decided that as I stood in the bathroom, sticking my white furry tongue out at the mirror.)

Gran was buzzing around as if she'd only had one glass of spring water the night before. "Really, Clare," she said, looking at me critically, "you'd better get a good breakfast inside you to line your stomach. I don't know what your father will say if you arrive back looking so ghostly!"

I thought that was bit rich considering that he might have got me back wearing handcuffs or been ordered to come and pay bail.

"Have you got a remedy for a hangover?" I asked.

"My remedies don't really work on *self-harm*," she said smugly, "but you could try some dock-and-rhubarb pills."

While she rang down for breakfast I took the medicine and massaged my forehead. There was a man playing bongo drums inside my right temple.

"You shouldn't have let me drink," I complained. "It's irresponsible of you."

"We're all responsible for ourselves," said Gran, "and we all have to learn the hard way. Now stop groaning and perk up. I'll need your help today."

"Where's Philippe?" I asked, dunking croissants in my hot chocolate and telling my stomach that it was going to like them.

"He stayed the night in Dan's room. They'll be here in a minute. We have to make a plan and the coach leaves in an hour."

I groaned inwardly. Not another plan. If asked, I would refuse to have anything to do with pliers. Gran was throwing windows open and emptying ashtrays. I wished she'd stop humming. She wasn't keeping rhythm with the bongos. Never mind, I thought, recalling the nice policeman; at least we avoided arrest.

"Did the policeman get a statement from Philippe?" I asked.

"A rough one. He agreed that Philippe can do a full written report in Ireland and send it to him. You know, I'd say there are lots of old people in many countries being ill-treated in homes like that one. I told the policeman that as far as I was concerned, we'd lifted the lid on a whole can of worms. Are you feeling sick?"

"Just a bit delicate." I'd had a sudden mental picture of a mass of seething maggot shapes. My stomach was grappling with the croissants and rumbling like a bad-tempered volcano. After a few minutes it decided that it wasn't going to erupt and settled down to sulk instead. The man was still going on the bongos but he was running out of energy. I started to feel half-human. It was beyond me why adults thought that drinking was pleasurable. Now I knew that Nuala Dunne was lying when she said that hangovers weren't that bad.

I got a little tickle of satisfaction when Bert, Peggy and Dan arrived. They looked delicate. I thought Bert might be hearing bongos from the way he winced when Gran squeaked the window, opening it wider. Philippe was with them, still looking tired but happy. He came over to me and kissed my hand. Normally I'd think that was gruesome but he wasn't a bit like a poser.

"Clare," he said, "I must congratulate you on last night's performance. You did a wonderful job keeping the policeman waiting. Bravo!"

"It was nothing," I said modestly.

"It was everything!" Philippe declared. "You were the kind of person I needed as a comrade in the dark days."

I liked that. It made me forget my hangover. I thought I could get used to having Philippe around. Nuala Dunne's grandfather hadn't been able to take part in the war (or so she said) because he had boils.

"The coach leaves soon," said Peggy. "What are we going to do about passport control at Dover?"

"And what about the others on the coach?" I said.

"They're going to notice an extra passenger."

"Maddy's taking care of that," Gran told us. "She's having a pow-wow with them in the breakfast-room and explaining what they need to know."

"But what if someone objects?" I asked. I couldn't stand the thought of anyone snitching on us.

"They won't," said Gran firmly, "I told you: Maddy's in charge."

I imagined Maddy's hand cutting dramatically across her throat and saw Gran's point. "What about Dover, then? How are we going to manage that?" I'd seen stuff on the TV about illegal immigrants being questioned for hours and kept in custody until they could be sent back. I didn't think Philippe would have the stamina for questioning. It was a long time since he'd stood up to the Gestapo. I found myself getting hot and cross when I thought that if we were found out he'd get sent back all on his own.

"I've been giving the matter some thought," Gran said, sitting with Philippe. "Grey power needs to strike again. Maddy's going to get Philippe a wheelchair. When we go through passport control I think that Dan should have another heart attack just in front of us and distract the officials. In the confusion we'll be able to slip through. I think you should push the wheelchair, Clare. A young girl with her poor old grandad won't be noticed."

Dan rubbed his head. "Does it have to be me again?" he asked pathetically. "I'm feeling a bit the worse for wear and the act's getting harder each time. Give us a break, Nora."

"Let me do it!" Peggy had perked up. "Look, I'm very

convincing!"

She started to stagger on the spot, clutching her chest and rolling her tongue. "Help, help!" she groaned, eyes staring. "It's...it's...my...aagh!" She sank to the floor and twitched.

I gave her a round of applause. "That's brilliant!"

Philippe nodded. "I think that all eyes will be on Peggy and her spasms."

Peggy was dusting her skirt. "Thanks," she said modestly. "I based it on my dying Ophelia. Of course, she drowned," she explained to me, "but it's the same technique. I wonder if Kenneth Brannagh would like to audition me?"

"I know about Ophelia," I said, offended. (I've read *Hamlet* in the comic version.)

"Right-o." Gran nodded. "As soon as people are buzzing around Peggy, you push Philippe away, Clare. Not too fast—you don't want to attract attention."

"I will pretend to be asleep," said Philippe. "If anyone speaks to me I will act deaf. I have never been to Ireland. This will be exciting!"

"It's God's own country," Dan assured him, "and the singing lounges are great."

"Are you sad to be leaving Belgium?" I asked Philippe.

He thought for a moment. "Yes and no. It is always sad to leave one's native country but I am glad to be reunited with the wonderful woman I have never forgotten. In Ireland I will have a family. Here I have only loneliness."

"Home is where the heart is," said Peggy soppily. "It's such a touching story."

Bert was looking misty-eyed too. He had his nose pressed to the window. I went over and looked down. Maddy was on the pavement outside the hotel, talking to the coach driver.

"What a woman," he said to me. "What a woman! D'you think she'd mind if I wrote to her? D'you think she might come and visit me in Ireland?" He cracked his knuckles anxiously.

"I think she likes you a lot," I said. "I'd write to her if I were you."

"Really? You think it would be the right thing?"

He was doing well for someone who'd started making enemies as soon as he'd stepped off the boat.

"Go for it, Bert," I told him. "Make sure you get her address." You never know, I thought, she might have a good-looking grandson.

Everyone else was on the coach by the time we climbed aboard. As Philippe reached the top of the steps there was a big cheer. "Grey power, grey power," came the chant. Clenched fists were raised. The coach driver seemed very nervous.

"It's OK," I reassured him. "They're not dangerous; they don't bite. It's just that they've had an exciting time."

"In *Brussels*," he said incredulously, looking at me as if I were crazy. "Excitement in *Brussels*? Where?"

I laughed. "I know! Unbelievable, isn't it?" If you only knew the half of it, I thought, smiling at his perplexed face.

Bert was standing on the steps, hopping on one foot, whispering to Maddy. She had her war-paint on again and his shoulders were getting covered with bits of her face. The coach driver couldn't shut the door. After five minutes people began to call to Bert. He and Maddy exchanged pieces of paper and he took his seat, blushing and fiddling with his peaked cap.

"Love is in the air!" someone shouted, and Bert pretended to be interested in a newspaper. As the coach pulled away Maddy was waving furiously and doing the can-can on the kerb. She caught my eye and gave a huge wink, pulling her hand across her throat....

There was a constant singsong all the way to Ostend. The coach driver had to stop once and request passengers not to dance in the aisles. We exchanged glances, the kind that teachers give each other at the end of a day out with their classes. I felt great sympathy for the poor man. There were people "singing" who'd been tone deaf since birth. Unfortunately, they had the loudest voices. I gave in to the man who was back playing the bongos and asked Gran for some more dock and rhubarb. She passed them to me with a bright smile and I wondered sourly if she was going to go around with that lunatic look on her face for the rest of her life.

It was frantic as we went through passport control. People were shoving and pushing. I didn't understand how they could actually look at anyone's passport in that throng, which was just as well as I'd discovered that trying to steer a wheelchair was about as easy as roller-skating over eggs without breaking them. I thought it would just be a matter of push and go but it was more a case of push, swerve, yank and groan. The thing was a dead weight and it had a mind of its own, like those supermarket trolleys that head side-ways for every aisle but the one you want to go down. Poor Philippe must have felt as if he was on a big dipper or in a car with a drunken driver. Sweat ran down the back of my neck as I tried to look as if I did this every day. Whenever I tried to forge ahead I lurched at an angle and bashed somebody's legs.

"Take it easy!" Gran hissed. "Don't go so fast!"

"It's not me," I snarled back, "this thing's self-pro-pelled! Where did Maddy get it from, a museum?"

We were approaching a uniformed man who was flicking his eye over passports. I tried to look innocent and sweet and fixed my gaze on Peggy's back, hoping that her timing was up to scratch. She didn't let us down. As the official reached for her passport she took a heaving breath and went into her whirling dervish act. There was immediate uproar. Peggy sounded as if she was being throttled. "Eergh, aargh, eergh!" I kept going, not too fast, while pandemonium reigned behind me. My muscles strained and complained as I tried to keep the wheelchair in a reasonably straight line, heading for the coach park.

At any moment I expected to hear a voice shouting, "Stop!" and a heavy hand to grip my shoulder. Arrested in charge of a drunken wheelchair! The world was spinning but suddenly I was through the doors and in the open air. The coach was in sight. My feet were treading in glue and my knees were starting to wobble. Soon I'd be a wheelchair case too.

"Bravo, Clare!" Philippe urged me on, keeping his head down. "Not far to go now. Don't think, just keep moving!"

"Keep moving," I repeated to myself. "Keep moving." My tongue seemed to be swelling in my mouth. I yanked the straying wheelchair back on course again. It whistled and creaked. Gran's hand came down on mine and helped me the last couple of yards.

"We've done it!" she said as she threw the wheelchair brake on.

"I'm done *in*," I protested, helping Philippe on to the coach before I collapsed next to him.

Gran poured half a bottle of Rescue Remedy down my throat. The others came hurrying on, clapping and smiling. An old man thumped Philippe on the back and started him coughing. In the distance came the sound of an ambulance siren.

"That's for Peggy," Bert said. "She'll have to spin them a convincing story. Dan's stayed with her. They'll get the train up to Holyhead and meet us there."

The coach moved away into the traffic. Philippe took a deep breath and touched my shoulder. "Thank you; you had a very difficult job."

"I feel as if all my muscles have been turned inside out," I told him. "That wheelchair should be scrapped." I looked sternly at him and Gran. "Do you realise that I, a young innocent person, have broken the law twice in twenty-four hours?"

Philippe looked at me gravely. "There are crimes and crimes," he said. "Every day there are terrible offences against humanity. I do not think that the little mischiefs you have done will be held against you. You have helped a very grateful old man to live his final years in peace and hope."

I choked up then. We all did. We shared my disgustingly grubby hanky as the coach sped away.

9

And Finally...

They all lived happily...
Well, who knows? There are some things you might like to know.

After we returned to Ireland we had one or two problems over Philippe's lack of papers but Gran's mafia—including some connections she had in high places—and the kind policeman in Brussels helped to sort it out.

Gran and Philippe got married two months after we got back. As Gran said, at their age they had no time to waste. We had a slap-up party: lots of Gran's international friends turned up with schnapps, vodka, sangria, retsina and lots of other drinks ending in "a". Mum broke off her meditating for a day and came along, although she wouldn't touch any alcohol. (She said it might interfere with her aura.) She and Dad went for a walk by the Percy French fountain and she agreed that we could go and visit her in Donegal.

Bert went back to Brussels within a couple of months to visit Maddy and came back sporting a beret.

Dan and Bert discovered that they shared a passion for country and western music and started to spend weekends together, listening to Tammy Wynette, Johnny Cash and Philomena Begley.

Bossy-Boots got two years in jail.

Miss Casey met Dan Burke's grandson, the travel agent, at Gran's wedding and they fell for each other. Luckily, Dan's grandson hasn't inherited his grandfather's taste in music.

Nuala Dunne broke a leg skiing and had to come home on a stretcher in the plane.

I never got round to entering the competition. My exercise books were still blank when I arrived back in Newcastle. I explained to Miss Casey that Brussels had been so exciting, I didn't get time to write a thing. She raised her eyebrows and said, "Brussels? Exciting?" I just don't understand why people have this strange idea that it's a boring place...

* * *